The Last Love Letter

Warren Holloway

Date: 4/23/19

FIC HOLLOWAY
Holloway, Warren,
The last love letter /

GOOD 2 GO PUBLISHING

The Last Love Letter

Written by Warren Holloway

Cover Design: Davida Baldwin – Odd Ball Designs

Typesetter: Mychea

ISBN: 978-1-947340-31-2

Copyright © 2018 Good2Go Publishing

Published 2018 by Good2Go Publishing

7311 W. Glass Lane • Laveen, AZ 85339

www.good2gopublishing.com

https://twitter.com/good2gobooks

G2G@good2gopublishing.com

www.facebook.com/good2gopublishing

www.instagram.com/good2gopublishing

The Last Love Letter

Chapter 1

Harrisburg, Pennsylvania
Present Day

Juan Dominguez, a young twenty-three-year-old Latino born in Puerto Rico but raised between Harrisburg and Philadelphia, was making another drug run.

He was on the rise in the cocaine game along with the rest of his team. He was known as "El Rey de Calle," or "the King of the Street," because of the flow of drugs he ran from Philly to Harrisburg. He flooded the different areas of the city, from the Southside projects, known as the South Acres, to the P-Funk projects.

Juan was unaware that his flow of drugs had drawn the attention of the local drug task force, who were watching him for the last week and two days.

Detective Monroe sat in his unmarked Crown Victoria about half a block away from Juan's low-key spot in the Cumberland Courts apartment complex, located in the uptown area of the city.

Detective Monroe, an Afro-American who stood six foot even, had a slim build, a bald head, and a full beard that was neatly trimmed. He was all too familiar with the street life, especially being raised in the Southside projects himself and witnessing drug transactions every day.

Juan was inside the apartment counting off his money that he needed to make the run down to his Mexican associates in Philly.

Once the count was totaled up, he tucked the $243,000 into a bag. There was enough to re-up and pay what he owed from the front, plus some extra to put up and then party with a little later that night.

Juan made a call to his Mexican associates

earlier in the day, so they already knew he was coming at a set time. Juan just needed to get there.

When he came outside with the book bag full of money over his shoulder, Detective Monroe was all eyes. He was simply waiting to give the signal to his task force buddies.

"He's coming out now and making his way to the all-white Mercedes. I believe it's an S55, so if he gets into the vehicle, we may have a chase on our hands," Detective Monroe said over the radio to his fellow officers.

Juan instinctively scanned the area, especially with the amount of money he was toting in the book bag.

He whipped out the remote and unlocked the doors as he approached the Mercedes.

"What you got in the bag?" Detective Monroe said aloud while looking over at Juan. "Get in the car!"

He knew if they stopped Juan in the car, they could also seize it for being used during the drug transaction.

Juan paused as he held the door handle on the car and took one more look around as if his instincts told him something was wrong.

But nothing.

He got into the Benz, started it up, and slipped a CD into the Alpine system. He was going to get his highway music ready and listen to a Large Flava mix CD.

He slipped the gear in reverse and backed out of the parking space, before he then made his way to the parking lot exit, all the while nodding his head to the music. But his head movement came to a halt when he saw the fast-approaching marked and unmarked police cars coming his way with their blue and red lights flashing. He could not hear the sirens over the loud music until he turned it down and saw that they had blocked him in.

"This is some real bullshit!" he yelled out.

He reached for his cell phone to call his associates in Philly and alert them to what was going on and tell them to never call the phone number again.

Juan removed the SIM card from the cell phone and destroyed it. He then broke the phone into pieces, so no one he had called or who had called him could be contacted.

Juan did not worry about the large quantity of money in the book bag. He was more focused on the Glock 40mm he kept in his waistline in case someone tried to rob him.

"Get out of the car with your hands up!" the police officers yelled while assisting the drug task force.

Detective Monroe walked over with his gun in hand and tapped on the passenger-side window with a smile.

"I gotcha, Juan! You going to jail now!"

Jail was the last place Juan wanted to go. Thoughts of shooting it out with the cops crossed his mind, especially after hearing the sarcasm in the detective's voice.

"Fuck you, cop! I'll be out by breakfast!"

Juan stepped out of the car with his hands up as the officers rushed over to secure his hands.

"You don't have to be so rough. It's not like I killed somebody!" Juan said, turning to see that it was a female officer along with a male officer placing the cuffs on him. "Then again, mami, you can play rough with me. You're probably into this shit anyway."

"Shut up, stupid! You have the right to remain silent." Her words faded into the blur of sirens wailing in the background.

Detective Monroe bragged and talked about the money he found as well as the discovery of the Glock 40 mm that he placed on the side of the seat.

"You're not getting out by breakfast, I hate to break that to you, unless you can afford a $1,000,000 bond!" Detective Monroe taunted Juan, knowing the district court judge would impose at least that amount of bond and not just 10 percent, because of the large amount of cash found.

Juan was overconfident, arrogant, and flamboyant.

"A million dollars in cash is nothing. My peoples would pay $2,000,000 if they had to, *cabron*. Like I said, I'll be out in the morning, and nena right here can cook me some scrambled eggs."

Detective Monroe nodded his head at the female officer, giving her the go-ahead to haul him off.

~ ~ ~

Three days passed by, and the reality of possession of a firearm, money laundering, and multiple counts of drug sales was starting to set in. This was due to the fact that most of his connects had changed their numbers, and his girlfriend claimed someone took the money that he had stashed away, which left him not wanting to trust her or anyone else.

Juan's bail was $1,500,000, no 10 percent. It was set so high because Detective Monroe made it clear to the district judge that Juan had bragged about making a high cash bail. Whoever came to pay that bail would, without question, be watched, questioned, and possibly indicted by the FBI. Knowing this made Juan's reality of spending time in jail something he needed to deal with.

Chapter 2

S ix months later, Juan was on the sheriff's bus heading up to CDCC Camp Hill State Prison with a sentence of eight and a half to seventeen years. This was something Juan never expected. He would have received less had he taken the plea bargain his public defender presented. Either way, he still would have ended up with a state sentence. Detective Monroe was all too happy seeing Juan off at the sentencing. He knew Juan would have no more chance to flood the streets with large amounts of cocaine; however, the detective still knew the war on drugs would always exist.

Juan looked on at the towers surrounding the state prison, along with the four razor-wire fences that would keep him and the other convicts contained.

Juan did not have anyone on the outside. His girl had betrayed him over the money she claimed someone had stolen, and his parents resided in Ponce, Puerto Rico. As for friends, no one had many when it came to places like this.

The sheriff's van came to a halt at the front of the oversized garage-door-like entrance that led into the sally port.

Juan took a look around once more. He knew it would be awhile before he stepped foot outside of the fences.

The sheriff's van was full of new commits as well as a few convicted parole violators (CPVs), who seemed to be happy to be back home. Many of them bragged about getting a good meal. However, there was nothing good about a meal being eaten in jail, Juan thought.

The sheriffs were met by corrections officers.

"You know the drill, men. Your guns will be placed in the lockboxes before entry."

The sheriffs exited the van and had their weapons secured before returning. As they exited the vehicle, the corrections officers walked around the van holding mirrors on long poles and looked underneath the van. They were followed by K-9s that sniffed around the van. The CDCC was maximum security and always on high alert.

Juan took in all the security measures. He knew he did not want to stay in a place like this for eight and a half long years.

"Bring 'em through!" the guard yelled out.

He was tall looking, like he could bench all the weights in the gym.

The van entered the sally port before coming to a halt. Then a slew of corrections officers came out and greeted everyone on the van.

"Get the hell out of the van! What you think this is, band camp?" the tall, muscular officer yelled, who was assisted by ten other officers.

"Stand in a straight line! You will not speak unless you're spoken to! We will not tolerate reckless eyeballing of our women that work here! You will come in and stand on the white line until your name is called!"

The officer was gripping a clipboard in his hand that contained everyone's information.

"Which one of you fags is Wilson?" his voice boomed through the air, after checking the names and charges on the list.

Wilson was an older gentleman about forty-six years old, who stood five foot five and weighed close to 250 pounds.

"I'm, I'm Wilson, sir," he responded timidly.

"You like to kill little kids, huh? You probably fondled them first, you fag!" The officer paused in speech as he approached Wilson face-to-face, almost as if they were ready to kiss. "You will not be killing anybody here! I should break you in half!" Spit came from the officer's mouth as he snapped while voicing his thoughts and emotions. "You want to try me? You think you can hurt me like you hurt those kids?"

Silence followed. Wilson was scared.

"I thought that would be your answer! As for the rest of you officers, get these scumbags out of my face!"

"You heard the sergeant! Get a move on!"

With all of the chaos and yelling, Juan was seriously thinking about his way out. This was not a lifestyle he planned on getting used to.

As the processing was underway, Juan scanned his surroundings and all the security features, which were top-of-the-line. He also looked on at the females working there.

When it came time for his photo ID to be taken, Juan decided he could have his way with words with the twenty-two-year-old intern.

"I've seen you before at Dragonfly nightclub," he said with a smile.

She did not say a word. She was trained to ignore these types of things, especially dealing with Pennsylvania's serial killers, drug dealers, serial rapists, and masterminds.

"What's your name, *nena?*" he said while leaning over out of view of the camera to take a glance at her nametag. "Melanie, huh?"

She cleared her throat before addressing what he needed to do. "Can you please look into the camera? Keep your feet on the yellow line."

"Anything for you, Melanie," he responded, looking around and making sure the guard was not near. "I need your help, nena. I can make you a lot of money, but you have to help me get out of here. He looked down at her shoes, hair, and nails. "You could use the money and spoil yourself."

She looked down at his name and immediately remembered the newspaper caption that mentioned all the money on him when he was arrested.

She was almost going to respond, when a correctional officer entered the room.

"Is this guy almost done here? We have another busload pulling in. We have to keep 'em moving."

"I was processing his photo for the ID. It should be coming out in a minute."

The impatient officer stood in the doorway, which compromised the conversation that was possibly about to go on.

Juan was anxious on the inside. His mind raced when he thought a possible opportunity was about to present itself, before the officer entered the room.

The ID intern made eye contact with Juan, which allowed him to know she was willing to entertain his proposal. She would have to hear if it was worth it. She was in the best position to manipulate the clearance codes on the IDs, and even change the parole date on the computer.

"Is that thing broke or something? It usually prints out those IDs pretty fast."

"It's not broken. It's printing the ID now. I just needed to fix a few things on the index for his printout," she responded with a bit of discouragement in her voice. "Here's your ID, Mr. Dominguez."

She handed him the ID with a note underneath it, which he immediately felt beneath the identification card. He quickly slid it into his pocket and then made his way out of the office.

"Take it into the next office. The counselor will be in there waiting to see you," the corrections officer said in a demanding tone, as if he was running a military boot camp.

Juan wanted to see what the note said. He did not want to see a counselor unless she was going to get him out of prison.

"Mr. Dominguez, right?" the counselor said as he entered.

"Yes, Juan Dominguez."

The thirty-two-year-old counselor was of Irish background, with red hair, a pale tone to her skin, and soft green eyes. But she weighed more than she wanted to, especially after she had her first baby. Although she would be able to bounce back, the pounds continued to add up, making her an easy 170 pounds, which was a lot for her five-foot frame. Being a single mom and working at a prison with a bunch of bad apples did not help her in the romance department. It made it easy not to fall for men, especially after interviewing them in the prison system every Monday through Friday.

But there was something about Juan's demeanor and his ability to grace a smile, especially considering the situation he was in. Maybe it was his way of bringing ease to the situation that he was trying to manipulate! Who knew! she wondered.

"I'm going to go over a list of questions to give me a better view of how to place you throughout the prison. This is what we call custody level, so I need you to be honest in answering these questions."

"I'm ready when you're ready," Juan responded with a smile, still anxious to get out of the room to read the note from the ID intern. "You didn't tell me your name."

"Ms. O'Conner. I'm a treatment specialist, counselor, or whatever it is you can remember me by."

"I'll remember your eyes since they glow."

She was taken aback by the random compliment and was unable to hold back the smile on her face. It had clearly been awhile since she heard such kind words. At the same time, she needed to remember where she was as well as who she was talking with: an inmate.

"Onto the questions, Mr. Dominguez. You were born in Puerto Rico and then raised in Philadelphia and Harrisburg. What about your parents?"

"Maria Dominguez, and my father, José, are both still in PR."

"Do you have any other siblings?"

"Maybe, but none that I know of."

She knew he really did not understand the question, which she thought was a little cute, although she did not allow him to read her thoughts.

"Do you have any brothers or sisters?"

"No, I'm the only one."

Ms. O'Conner continued on with her questions and found out more about Juan. He was a unique case. He could have easily been in marketing with his networking skills selling drugs. Had he met with the proper legal team, he probably would not have been in the place he was today.

"Are there any questions you have that you would like to ask me about your stay here at the CDCC?"

Juan was smooth. His smile lit up as his thoughts processed, and he prepared for the delivery.

He glanced toward the door to make sure the correctional officer was not coming in to put the rush on him like he did with the young woman in the ID office.

"If it was another time or another place, would you take me seriously or appreciate the fact that my compliments of your natural beauty are sincere?"

Juan definitely had a way with words. Poetry came naturally to him. It was something he did in high school to get girls, even in his first year of community college before he dropped out to pursue the more lucrative lifestyle of selling drugs.

Ms. O'Conner was almost speechless, but she definitely appreciated the attention. She was even getting butterflies in her stomach. She did not know if it was because of her position, or if she was in fear of losing her job if caught speaking with the inmate on terms outside of the paperwork in front of her. The feeling was good, but it was unethical. She did not want to lose her job, and she knew that she had a six-year-old at home that depended on her.

"I wish I could answer your question, Mr. Dominguez, but since I can't, we're done here," she responded, before standing up from her seat.

Her eyes glowed as she tried to hold back a smile, almost feeling as if something good had just happened. But she knew she had to let it slip away, and it did just that as he walked out of her office.

He returned to the reality of Camp Hill Prison as soon as he stepped outside her office door.

Officers were yelling at the other inmates, which was their way of trying to impose scare tactics so that no one would get out of line in their stay at the CDCC.

"Hey, dumb ass! Dominguez! Whatever your damn name is. Take it in that room right there until you're called again!" the officer yelled out.

Juan made his way into a cell with six other inmates that were processed just as he was. He made his way over to the bathroom area, which provided partial privacy with a four-foot wall.

He took out the note from his pocket. He was interested to see what Melanie had written.

The note read: *Freedom costs!* Underneath it was a dollar amount: *$150,000.*

She figured he could at least afford that

amount, since he was caught with an even higher sum, especially if he wanted his freedom. Melanie also needed the money to pay off her student loans, car loan, rent, and credit card debts. She also wanted to splurge a bit and treat herself to some shopping.

"Greedy bitch!" Juan voiced lowly upon seeing what she had written down.

He did not have the money, but she did not know that, so he planned on leading her on to get what he needed: his freedom.

Juan made his way back to the locked door and stared out the window at the other inmates walking in and out of various rooms, along with the correctional officers yelling out orders. He did not take his eyes off the ID office. He wanted to make eye contact with Melanie to give her the okay about the note.

He stood there for close to an hour before she popped out for her lunch break.

His heart pounded in excitement as his mind raced while thinking about his freedom.

When Melanie walked by the large cell in which Juan was held, he tapped on the glass to get her attention. When she turned toward the sound, she saw that it was Juan. He gave her the thumbs-up with his signature smile, manipulating her for what he needed. She, too, was using him under the pretense that she was going to be rewarded with $150,000. Her greed and desire to pay off bills gave her the much-needed incentive—that and not wanting to be around the yelling guards all day. It was not a healthy work environment for someone like her, who was easy going and gentle.

Melanie turned her head forward now thinking of what she needed to do to get him released. There were so many different ways that she could manipulate the computer's actual files on Juan Dominguez. This was something she would think about while on her lunch break.

Juan stepped away from the door and made his way back over to the bathroom, only to pull out the note and glance at it once more time. He then ripped it up and tossed it into the toilet to be flushed.

"Dominguez! Wilson! Jackson! Holland! Anderson! Wallace! You idiots come out and grab the box with your name and number on it. Then get back in line until the officer tells you otherwise!" the correctional officer's voice boomed, sounding off through the intercom at the front of the large cell.

His voice was followed by a buzzing sound that unlocked the door.

Officers were on the outside of the door ready to keep things moving along.

"Get your box as you were told. Don't make this harder than it should be. You know your name and number, so grab the one with your name and number, or I will slam your face forward on the box that belongs to you, so you don't forget which one is yours!"

Juan did not want to leave just yet. He wanted to stay in the cell to find out what Melanie was going to do or could do for him. This process was moving faster than he expected. It also seemed to ruin his chances of getting out, and that in itself was not good. He knew he needed to maximize on every opportunity.

Juan was so into his thoughts that he did not realize that the line in front of him was moving, until the guard's voice sounded off.

"Hey, asshole! Your feet glued to the floor?"

"No, sir, I didn't know we were moving," Juan responded without making eye contact, because it could be construed as a challenge, or his words could be taken as sarcasm.

This was something he learned while in

college taking social skills psychology.

Juan put a move on it and joined the rest of the inmates who were escorted by the officers.

"In case you morons didn't notice, you are not at home. This is my house. You follow my rules. You have a rule manual. While on R-block, you retards are expected to read these rules to make yourself familiar with being here at Camp Hill. There will be an orientation to explain further. Until then, do as you're told. Now let's go."

All of the inmates in the CDCC wore blue jeans and light blue shirts. Only the inmates classified at Camp Hill prison wore browns.

As they were making their way to R-block, Juan spotted Melanie coming from the ODR officer's dining room. He wanted to make eye contact with her, so she would know that he was on the move, but she stopped to talk to another employee on the walkway.

Juan did not take his eyes off of her. He wanted them both to be on the same page; while at the same time, he wanted to make sure she took care of things and got him out of jail.

As those thoughts ran across his mind, she parted ways with the employee she was speaking with. Juan was desperate, so he raised his hand and waved at her. He was unaware of all the security throughout the prison, the eight guard towers, the center tower over control, and the security booth in the middle of the crosswalk as well as all the officers walking around.

The line came to a halt. By this time, Melanie saw Juan at the same time the officer spotted him waving her down.

"Hey, jackass! What do you think this is, Cinco de Mayo and we're in a parade!"

Melanie heard the guard yell at Juan and simply continued on, not wanting to get caught up. At the same time, she knew she had bigger plans and money to make.

"I don't think this is a parade or Cinco de Mayo. I was fixing my shirt."

"I see right now, CO Davis, we may have to keep an eye on this one. He's real slick. Now get to the front of the line so CO Davis can keep you at his side."

Juan moved quickly but wondered if he just had blown his chances to get out. As he was having those thoughts, Melanie was also having thoughts of making money. But she knew she would have to wait for the opportunity to manipulate the computers to show a new minimum date for Juan Dominguez without compromising herself.

*T*hree days went by, and there was still no sign of Melanie playing her part in assisting Juan with his freedom.

Juan was in a cell on R-block. His cellmate was Tre, a Crypt gang member from the north side of Pittsburgh. He was in for shooting at the cops after a long car chase after doing a drive-by on another set. Juan thought he had a lot of time until he met Tre, who was working with a twenty-five-to-fifty-year sentence. He would be close to fifty when he got out if he made parole the first time around. Juan listened to his gang stories over and over for the three days they were in the cell together, but Juan's main focus was seeing Melanie and staying in her head about his escape.

As he stared, he hoped he would see her pass

by so he could bang on the window to get her attention, but nothing. There was no sight of her.

Juan did not tell Tre too much about himself. He knew better than to be so open about his case, even though he was already sentenced. However, he did give him bits and pieces of what had taken place, mainly the large amount of money he was trapped with. Juan still could not believe that he did not have anything to show for it. Memories were all he was left with. It was like an excerpt from one of Young Jeezy's songs: "Ball til we fall, go to jail and talk about it all."

"Dominguez!" a voice yelled from behind him, pulling him away from the window out of which he was staring.

When he turned to see that it was the CO sliding mail through the door, he was anxious to see who was writing, especially since everybody he showed love to out on the streets seemed to have left him hanging.

He came to the gate and found two letters addressed to him. The first letter was from someone he never expected would write to him. It was his ex-girlfriend, Deja, from the South Acres projects. He had given his Spanish mami the world, and she had stolen it from him, so seeing her name stirred up some old emotions.

"You got some love, huh?" Tre said after seeing that Juan had received mail.

"A two-piece. One's from my old chick; the other is some broad named Mel B. I don't know who it is, but I'm about to find out after I see what my ex is talking about."

Juan opened Deja's letter and saw that there were two pictures inside, both of her striking sexy poses in her lingerie. Seeing her in the baby-blue lace made him flash back to when they were on the best of terms. She was looking good in the pictures, with her sexy hazel brown eyes and the mole above her mouth on the right side. Her salacious poses almost made him forget about the $100,000+ that she had stolen from him. He moved on, unfolding the letter to read what she really had to say.

April 9, Saturday
Dear Juan:

It's been awhile since I last talked to you, papi. I know you mad as hell at me. My stupid-ass family put me up to that bullshit. Damn, I miss you, papi! I hope you can forgive me. I hope you like these pictures. I did this for you. Another thing, papi, I still have some of the money. There's like $47,000. It took me some time to count it last night, but I'll hold on to it. I promise as long as you're not mad.

Love always,
Deja—Your boo

After reading her letter, his thoughts and emotions were mixed once more. He was happy that she had some of his money, which meant he needed to figure out a way to get it. He was also pissed that she lied to him in the beginning by saying she was robbed for close to $150,000.

He knew without question he was going to have to apply his charm in many ways to get his money while entertaining Deja, appeasing her heart and mind.

"Yo, Tre, my ex is crazy. She hit me for almost 150, tells me that she got robbed, and now she sends these flicks talking about she's sorry but still has some of my paper."

Tre leered at the pictures and saw how sexy Deja looked. She could easily pass for a *King* magazine model or a video vixen in Jay-Z's "Big Pimpin'" video.

"Yeah, you got something official right there, Ike," Tre said as he handed the pictures back. "But I would have slumped her for a $150, Ike."

"Trust me, she knew I couldn't get to her, plus she said her family put her on to this shit."

"Get the rest of your ones before she spends

that shit, Ike."

"I'm gonna be on that letter as soon as I get done reading this other one."

Juan took another look at the name on the envelope: Mel B. He still could not figure out who this was. He didn't recognize the name or the New Cumberland address.

April 8, Friday

Hey mi amigo:

You probably thought I forgot about you? I couldn't take care of that today. There were too many people around. Don't worry! I'm working on it. Just make sure you have the money.

Sincerely,
Your secret associate, Mel B :)

He could not help but laugh aloud upon seeing that Melanie took the initiative to get his information to write, which in itself was a risk for her.

"What you trippin' on, Ike?" Tre asked.

"Nothing! This broad's crazy. You know how they be?"

"I hear you. Just get your paper from that one chick, because she's sexy. But she ain't worth that paper, Ike."

"Ike" was a Pittsburgh saying, and something Tre said a lot when addressing people.

Juan was now in game mode. He was ready to respond to the letters he just had received. First was Melanie.

Melanie was five foot three and 120 pounds, and she had no kids. She was from an Italian background, with black hair, a natural tan to her radiant skin tone, and innocent light brown eyes. Her true beauty was played down from always working. She never really had a chance to get dolled up like her girlfriends with whom she grew up. They had more means and access to money. Now Melanie figured she could have a little taste of pleasure, indulging in the good life with no debt and giving her the financial freedom to roam as she pleased.

Juan sat at the desk in the cell with pen in hand. He was ready to get the ball moving.

Hey Beautiful:

First, let me start off by thanking you for not just taking the time to reach out to me, but placing yourself and job on the line at the same time. It says a lot about your drive. Every good man needs someone like you at his side. I guess that would make me lucky, having you holding me down as you are, although the reason has its means. Speaking of which, I'll have something sent to you, which should give you more incentive to make things happen. Take care, beautiful.

Truly,
Your secret associate

Juan kept it brief. He did not want to give too much in the first letter. He also wanted to feel her out, even though she was already at the point of being managed and/or manipulated.

The next letter Juan needed to write was to Deja. He figured if he talked the love story stuff to her, she would he back where he needed her to be.

Deja,

Que pasa, nena? Hola, como esta? *I can't lie, I miss you more than words can explain. This time away has allowed me to realize the good I had being free, the good that came when it was just you and me. You did what you did with the money, and as you can see, most of it is gone. But look, you're still here, and the love in your heart for me has never faded. Everything happens for a reason. As you can see, you found your way back to me, back to the house of love, and the same place your heart calls home, or should I say your comfort zone? Damn, mami! Seeing you in those sexy photos made me miss making love to you. You know all the freaky shit we was into? Yeah, we going to be good, nena. Just keep that money away from your family. We can use that for our future crib together. I can do a lot with that to get things back to where they used to be, and we can move wherever you like. Since I'm on that money talk, I need you to take $5,000 to the* *address on the back of this letter, but don't ask no questions. This is for me to come home early, so that's all you need to know, mami. Also send me a stack for my books, so I can go to the store when they have it. Before I close this out, I want you to know that I can't wait to see you face-to-face. We going to do it big. I'ma take you to Puerto Rico and show you my hood back home, and then to the beautiful side of PR—the same side I want to make love to you on. It's a thought, so keep it in mind. Take care, nena.*

Love,

Juan

The letters were done, and everything was coming together. Deja was back on the scene with some of the money, and Melanie's greed was going to get the best of her. She was not prepared for what was to come. Juan wanted to wet her beak a little, giving her the $5,000. He knew she never had that amount of money; and it was going to be in cash, all $20 bills in $1,000 intervals, wrapped in rubber bands, fifty $20s per rubber band, five stacks in total. When she got the money in her hand, a certain feeling would take over her. It would be freedom, power, euphoria, and a sense of winning the lottery. Although she wanted $150,000, the $5,000 would make her feel like she had $50,000, especially all in cash.

Juan climbed to the top bunk and lay back while staring at the ceiling. He thought out his plans to live on the outside of the fences that contained him. He knew he could not stick around there any longer.

Chapter 4

A total of seven days passed by since Juan stepped foot in the CDCC at Camp Hill. He was now among the other level threes and fours roaming the yard and looking for an out, legally or illegally. At the same time, he reflected on the lives they used to live outside of the four fences that surrounded them.

Juan's old cellmate, Tre, also made his way into the population running wild with his Crypt homies. They tried to catch Bloods slipping or anyone that wasn't in their set.

Juan spoke to a few people with whom he came through classification, but it was about nothing in depth. He was more focused on getting out. All he could think of was Melanie taking care of business, and Deja making sure she took that money over to her, which would give her the much-needed incentive to get things moving.

He strolled around the yard in thought while keeping an eye alert for anyone trying to get at him with a knife or just wanting to fight as a way to be made a member in the growing gang population.

"Yard in! Yard in! Take it back to your blocks!" the guard yelled over the intercom before grabbing his shotgun and standing firm.

He made sure no one attempted to break out or start a riot at the last minute, which was something that Camp Hill was known for when they had a three-day riot in the late 1980s.

Juan knew to take to the back of the line or be first, something he was told in the county. Never mix in, because it leaves opportunity for an enemy to attack.

He waited to the end of the line before making his way into the cell block and headed directly to his cell as the rules stated.

Mail awaited him on the cell floor. He had two letters again. One was from Deja, and the other was from Melanie. There was also a call-out slip from his counselor, Ms. O'Conner, dated for the following day.

Juan's new cellmate was from Juarez, Mexico. He came through Pennsylvania taking care of business but had to shoot someone over a package. He was now spending seven and a half to fifteen years in prison for aggravated assault.

Puto's English wasn't that clear, but he spoke in broken English, which was good enough to be understood when he wanted to. Puto jumped up on the bunk with his drawing pad while Juan got into his mail. He was anxious to see what the holdup was, while at the same time, he was hoping that the ball was still rolling.

He first opened Deja's letter.

April 14, Thursday

Hey Papi:

I had a dream about you last night. Mmmmmh, I wish I could have recorded that shit; it was sexy and good. Damn, I miss you, papi! I can't wait to see you face-to-face again. I can't lie. Reading your letter and knowing you still love me and forgive me made me want to never leave your side and hold you down, no matter what. We've been through a lot. As you said, we came back to love. Money isn't everything; love means the world. You are my world, papi. I got the pictures of you and me all over the apartment; therefore, whenever I want to see your face, or whenever I miss you, I just turn and look to see your eyes looking back at me. It gives me comfort, even though I want the real thing. I guess I'll have to settle for the photos and your letters to keep me company until I get there, and the good dreams like I had last night. I woke up satisfied. Papi, I did take care of that money thing with blanquita. She was nervous and happy all in one. She wanted to talk, but I didn't want to get to know her, since I know this is business to get you here with me. You better not trip on me for blanquita! I know you love this good-good. Take care, papi, and know I love you and think about you every day. Anything you need just let me know.

Love always,
Deja/Tu amor

Juan was feeling good about the money being handed over to Melanie; and more importantly, he loved the fact that he had a strong emotional grip on Deja. He had her right where she needed to be. He also planned on maximizing her use until he managed to get out. Deja was not all bad; she just had done enough damage to compromise the trust and love between them. Her running away with the money left him without the financial means to afford a private attorney who would have done better in negotiating a lesser plea deal for him.

Deja's scent was on the letter. She had sprayed it heavily. It was J.Lo Glow, her favorite. Juan took the envelope and smelled the fragrance that took him back to when the times were good between him and Deja. The moment of pleasure was interrupted when the guard's voice came over the intercom, which brought him back to the reality of being in jail.

"Pill line! Pill line!"

The announcement did not apply to him, only those seeking to medicate themselves to get past the pain of being incarcerated. That and those loving to stay high.

He focused back on the second letter, which was from Melanie.

April 13, Wednesday

Hey amigo,

OMG, I thank you so much for the money! I couldn't wait to get back to work, so I could take care of things. I know you probably wanted an immediate release date, but that would have drawn red flags across the board. So what I did was override the computer to make your minimum control date in five and a half months since you almost got seven in now. This will also give you the

time needed to forward the remaining $145,000 to me.
Oh, your girl is pretty, which allows me to know what
your type is. Anyway, if you need anything else, let me
know. Bye-bye for now.

Sincerely,
Your secret associate, Mel B

"Yes, that's what I'm talking about!" Juan said to himself in a low tone.

He was feeling the power and control once again. He was close to being back on the streets and being the king of the streets once more. There was only one downside: he needed to produce the rest of the money before Melanie went back into the computer to change the time back to its original form. It was something he did not doubt she could do, which made his mind race to find a resolution to this situation.

Melanie was open and having a taste of pleasure with the money. However, at the same time, she had seen Deja, which allowed her to know the caliber of woman that Juan dealt with. So, naturally, she tossed out her thoughts to Juan in the letter, which made him take a mental note, something he planned to use to his advantage.

Hey beautiful:

I got your letter today, clearly making me feel good inside and out, knowing you took care of business and are a woman of her word. Once again, you proved to me your strength. It also makes me wonder how someone such as yourself with so many outstanding qualities can be without a man to appreciate all the good in you. You don't have to answer this since we are on business terms; however, to make it clear to you, Deja is a friend from my past. She's holding my money down as you can see. Now, realistically, you have what a man yearns for. Your smile is welcoming, even when you're trying to hold it back. It was something I noticed when flirting with you in the ID office. Your eyes tell a story. I see someone who needs comfort and that one you can turn to. Your true beauty is hidden behind the uniform you have to wear, but in my mind, I see you in another light, outside of here.

So when it comes to my type as you said, I see you, and I see something I can appreciate—something nice. We can take advantage of this situation that has been presented to us since we have five and a half months to get to know one another a little more. You can view it as a test drive. You'll be able to see who I am besides what you've read in the headlines, or what the paperwork says about me. Then again, you may be thinking on the lines of just keeping it business? I don't know. Just get back to me on that. I'll do the same with the money, to make sure we secure each end of the business.

Your secret associate

Juan was really into his thoughts, finding himself not just trying to influence Melanie's mind and heart to flow along as he wished, but also really entertaining his own words as they formed on the paper. He was thinking that it could be a new start. Maybe his curse of being incarcerated may have turned into a blessing?

He turned around and looked out the window to see the kitchen workers returning to the block, along with those who went to pill line. They were all moving a little slower than they were before they raced out of the block.

"Five minutes to count! This is your five-minute warning to count!" the officer yelled over the intercom, another reminder of being in jail.

Juan then focused back on grabbing Deja's letter. He smelled it again before responding to her.

Deja:

What up, mami? It feels good having you back in my corner. A part of me was lost without you, and that same part was beginning to turn cold until you came back into my life and allowed me to know that true romance and love does exist. I was thinking about you and me becoming a little closer throughout the time I'll be here, which isn't for long. We can rebuild on the love and trust that we did lose. I'm ready to listen to you and your heart, so that I know what is needed to keep you happy. View it as falling in love again, something we'll both enjoy. Like in your letter, you can tell me about your dreams. Things like this will strengthen our bond, our love, our trust, and our relationship. I want you to feel my presence. As you said, you have the pictures, so I want you to feel me in each room. Close your eyes, feel me next to you, and visualize me making love to you and getting the best of you. Deja, tu eres todo lo que necesita en mi vida para siempre. Yo quiero que seas mia. Yo solo te quiero ati. *I say this* pare de corazon, por que, blanquita es no importa. *Mami, it's about you and me now. It's time to settle down. I want what Will and Jada or Jay-Z and Beyoncé have. I want their money, too, but that's another thing we can work on together. With that said, nena, take care. Keep me in mind and closer to your heart. One more thing, I love your perfume. It reminds me of the good times.*

*Love Juan—*Tu amor para siempre

After Juan was finished with the letters, he sealed them up to be dropped in the mail. He was feeling good about all the dominos falling in place. He knew he needed to stay up on Melanie and Deja. This string of letters was just the beginning of his plan. He needed to make sure he did not deplete his funds with Deja. All he knew was selling drugs to make quick flips with the money, which was his next move: to get Deja to flip some of his money, so he could pay Melanie the full $150,000 if he could. The backup plan to that was to somehow lure Melanie in on the emotional love thing, so she did not feel a need to want all of the money as long as she had him.

For Juan to only be twenty-three years old, he was precocious, without question, and he possessed the ability to deceive or manipulate all those who came in contact with him, especially if he somehow benefited from it. It was the nature of the beast and instinctive to him, and it also helped him weed out the good from the bad.

Chapter 5

Juan made his way to Ms. O'Conner's office at 9:45 a.m. She was filling in for the H-block counselor that day, so Juan needed to go to the office on a different block.

She secretly lit up when he arrived at the door, reflecting back on the compliment that he had given her over a week ago.

"Mr. Dominguez, come in and take a seat right there," she said, taking her eye off of him and then looking down at the papers in front of her. "I called you in today to go over your paperwork and treatment plan while you're here in the DOC. Just a few things you'll need to make parole in five and half months."

She suddenly stopped looking at the date on the paper. She felt that something was not right about it. She remembered him clearly from the flirting, the amount of time he would have to serve, and the quantity of money. "Maybe this is the wrong paperwork," she added, checking to see if he would refute what she was saying.

"You're funny and beautiful. It makes being around you even more welcoming," he replied, sending a compliment to divert her attention.

He sensed her willingness to cross that unethical line. Besides, the odds were in his favor. Three out of four staff members at one point or another establishes a personal or intimate relationship with an inmate, whether it be for sexual favors assisting escape, or running illegal packages into the prison.

She was taken back once again by his suave approach to everything, knowing his flirtatious ways could easily get him a DC-141, or misconduct, and place him in the restricted housing unit (RHU). This level of intrigue added to the gravitational pull that surrounded Juan and lured her in.

"Maybe it's just all of the people I see. I could have easily gotten you mixed up with someone else."

She wasn't a good liar; however, she decided on her own to check up on this later. However, right now, she was enjoying Juan's presence while picking his mind apart.

"So what type of programs do you think will help you transition back to the streets in five and a half months?"

"I don't have any addictions. Selling drugs isn't something I have to do. It's something I chose to do. I have a few more credits left to get my degree in psychology, and I'm also good with my hands."

A sexual thought crossed her mind for some strange reason. Was it how he said he was good with his hands? Or maybe it was the fact that she had been sex deprived for five long years and pleasuring herself was no longer enough. But she did not want to give herself away to anyone. She wanted love and something special, but her work consumed her, as did being a mother and her second job.

A brief smile slipped across her face before speaking. "What exactly is it you do good with your hands, Mr. Dominguez?"

"I'm a jack of all trades. I'm familiar with anything that needs to be fixed in the house or on the car. I learned all of this growing up. I read about everything like electricity and other stuff, which fascinated me as a child."

Upon hearing his response and his ability to fix things around the house, she was thinking more about him fixing all of her needs, sexually and emotionally. Her mind raced with visions as she briefly fantasized about her and Juan outside of the prison. She could see him at her place, in her bed, and in her life. But she quickly snapped back to the reality of the moment and realized that she was too afraid to cross the line. She needed her job—the same job that engulfed her and deprived her of everything she wanted and yearned for.

"Mr. Dominguez, I'm going to put you down for a group called Thinking for a Change, as well as the organization named Alcohol and Other Drugs (AOD). You'll learn from them, and hopefully these groups will assist you in your stay here and in life after you leave here."

"How long are these programs?" Juan questioned, remembering talk in the yard about programs being long and interfering with parole.

"Each program is twelve weeks. I'll place you on the list immediately. Now if you get processed and sent to your new jail, the counselor there will place you on the list in that prison," she informed him, pausing while typing in the information on the computer for Juan to be placed in the groups. "It's done. Do you have any questions for me?"

She remembered the first time she asked this and the question he asked. Now she was almost hoping for something along the lines of such.

"Mr. Sinclaire is the normal counselor for this block, right?"

"Yes, he is. He's off today, but he's scheduled to return tomorrow."

"Opportunity presents itself, or fate. Something meant to be, can't be avoided. It's inevitable, so why is it? I was ready to walk out of here as if the chemistry wasn't permeating through our words, gestures, or thoughts. I'm not saying that I know what you're thinking, but I can't be far off. Call it instinct, but why do we resist?"

If the attraction was not there, he would be in handcuffs finishing his poetic speech in the RHU. Ms. O'Conner embraced every word that flowed from his mouth. They were sweet to hear, almost like foreplay. Although a part of her was still resisting, a fraction of her wanted to bring balance to the situation.

Juan's course on psychology was working. He was reading her body language and facial gestures while listening to the pattern of her voice as she spoke. Although he sensed some resistance, at the same time, he could see right through the glass wall of protection behind which she was hiding.

"This is clearly a difficult situation, Mr. Dominguez."

"Juan. Please call me Juan, since we're addressing a more intimate and personal subject. That's if we're going to continue this conversation, Dawn?"

She was surprised that he said her first name. It was another of his ploys to lure her into the web of deceit, or was this the real thing for him?

"In my five years of working here, Juan, I've never had someone come on to me, let alone compliment me as you do. In fact, my life outside of here is spent raising my daughter. I don't have time for a relationship, because of my work schedule. Besides, I don't want to lose my job. How would I be able to take care of my baby?"

Juan heard enough. He was ready to seize what he viewed as the perfect opportunity. This was different than the communication he was having with Melanie. They have a business relationship all about money, but this was different; there was something there. Juan's motives and means were like an artifice that even confused him at times, but there was something unique about Dawn.

"I respect you, Dawn, as a working woman and mother. In fact, I commend you on your strength, doing what you do without the help of a man. Dawn, my intentions aren't to compromise your life or work schedule or jeopardize your means of income. We can have the sub rosa lifestyle while I'm here and keep what is between us just between us. Kind of like Vegas. What happens there stays there. Nobody needs to know other than you, which adds to the intrigue, making you and I appreciate what we have or will have between us."

She smiled freely and no longer tried to hold it back, and even if she was, it was not working. His words provided a sense of pleasure and euphoria, like listening to her favorite love song, but she still came back to the reality of the situation they were in.

"Juan, let me think about this. You'll know if it's a yes or no. Now that we have that out of the way, Mr. Dominguez, I'll sign your pass and you can go back to your cell."

As she slid the pass over the desk, his hand touched hers, sending a sensation rushing through her body as if igniting hidden emotions or a first kiss. She looked into his eyes and wanted to be closer. She wanted to know if everything he was saying was real, and she wanted to know if she did let him in, how would their love story end?

"Have a nice day, Ms. O'Conner."

"You too, sir," she replied as his hand slid off of hers.

She was already having a nice day entertaining the proposal that Juan left behind. There was something about being pulled closer to something that she was not supposed to have. It was Eve in the Garden of Eden. She simply wanted a taste of pleasure, to feel and be loved, and the risk that came with it added to the torturous emotions and thoughts she was having.

Chapter 6

At 4:06 p.m., Dawn O'Conner was placing her things into the trunk of her car in the parking lot of the prison. She was ready to go home after a long day at work, only to finish out the day at home with her daughter, Breeana. Bree was at the afterschool daycare center, so Dawn needed to rush over and pick her up, head home, and then plan what was for dinner.

As she drove to the daycare, weaving in and out of the 4:00 p.m. rush-hour traffic, she thought about her day—mainly her encounter with Juan. It was the highlight of her day. She meant to check up on his file, to see if there was a computer error, but she was sidetracked by his proposal and working on other caseloads.

She was thinking about his hand gracing across hers at the end of their intimate conversation; and once again, the thoughts alone brought a smile to her face. She was in a daze visualizing life with Juan. Her visions were of them spending time together, him making her laugh and being the man that she was missing, him making love to her body and placing random kisses over her body, his gentle yet manly touch, his presence, and his love inside of her both physically and emotionally. She was so wrapped up in her thoughts, smiling the whole time as if she was in a movie—a true romance—between her and Juan. It was picture-perfect, or it was until she heard her daughter calling out her name.

"Mommy! Mommy!"

She did not even realize how far gone she was into her thoughts. She had driven cautiously to the daycare with her eyes wide open, yet her mind was on Juan from the time she left the prison to when she arrived at the daycare. She was lost in the fantasy lifestyle she wanted to have with Juan. But it would be just that until she decided to cross the unethical line and make her fantasies and daydreams a reality.

She turned to her daughter with a smile as the thoughts dissipated somewhat yet still lingered.

"Hey, honey, how was your day?"

"Fun! Fun and fine."

"Sounds almost as good as Mommy's day."

"So that's why you're smiling? I thought you were happy to see me."

"I am happy to see you, Bree. Mommy was just happy about some other things that were going on, too, but not as important as you, honey."

"My day was fun. This boy in my classroom likes me. He said I'm pretty, Mommy."

"You are pretty, honey; and when you get old enough, you can have a boyfriend, but not until then."

Breeana was too cute. She was a miniature version of her mother, but her happiness came from child's play, or puppy love, if one could even call it that. This was definitely something she would laugh at when she got older.

"Bree, you want McDonald's or Burger King?" Dawn asked, not wanting to cook that night.

She just wanted to take a shower and watch her shows while Breeana played with her toys and watched her shows on Cartoon Network.

"McDonald's, Mommy. I don't want a kids' meal. I want a Big Mac, fries, and Coke."

"Whatever you want, honey," Dawn replied, noticing her baby girl trying to make adult changes by wanting the Big Mac versus the kids' meal.

Maybe it was her little boy toy at school that made her feel happy inside and out. Then again, she was only a child, and this moment in time would cause a laugh in the future.

As Dawn drove to get the food, she opted for the Asian salad and bottled water. Normally she would make Bree wait until they were at home before she indulged, but this time, she bent the rules a little.

"You can eat some of your fries, Bree, if you want."

"Okay, Mommy," she said as she reached into the bag, glad that she did not have to sneak a fry out of the bag like she normally did. Fresh hot fries tasted so good. "Mmm, good!" she added.

It did not take long before they arrived at their Oxford Manor apartment in Mechanicsburg, Pennsylvania, which was approximately fifteen minutes from the prison.

Dawn worked hard to keep her two-bedroom apartment. Times were difficult paying $750 a month for rent, not including utilities or the other bills she worked so hard to maintain. But it was worth having their own comfortable space.

Her place was decorated with tan leather couches and a few paintings to complement the gold-plated fixtures around the living room and dining room. Bree's bedroom was Dora themed. It was her playground. As for Dawn's bedroom, it was a continuous flow of tan and gold-plated furniture.

Bree ate her dinner before Dawn washed her up and sent her off to her bedroom to do what she did best: play and watch cartoons.

Dawn was in the shower allowing the steam to fill up as the hot water beat down on her flesh, massaging her body and releasing the stress and tension of the workday. Thoughts of Juan crossed her mind. The conversation they had earlier in the day once again brought a smile to her face. She was now entertaining the thought of allowing him into her life. The thoughts and visions she began to have caused her to slip into the place of fantasy once again, visualizing coming home to Juan with dinner on the table— something special he prepared.

After dinner, a movie; and after the movie, a little adult dessert of foreplay, with his gentle hands touching her in places her body yearned for, for so long. Kisses would be placed not only against her soft lips, but also to her neck, a spot that was her trigger, which caused her to moan in heat wanting more of him. Then his kisses would slide down to her breasts as his hands gently groped each of them.

Her clothes came off, and his followed. The moment of passion she had been neglecting for five years had now come. She whispered words to him to be gentle, something he was already doing while making her body feel loved, cherished, and appreciated to the fullest. His kisses picked up where they left off just below the belly button. Her legs willingly parted, since she wanted what was next. A taste of vanilla pleasure followed. His tongue was good for more than talking, and her body was loving all of him yet begging for him to get on top. His eyes connected with hers, followed by a passionate kiss as he slid into her tight and warm love spot. It was perfection at its best. She sighed in passion and love, enjoying what was happening to her. She was heating up as the sensation was taking over her body. She could not hold back anymore. She was ready to explode. Her legs were trembling, and she was experiencing mult-iples.

"Juan, Juan! You make me feel good!" she spoke, almost gasping sexually as her body continued to release.

She could feel his embrace, even his kisses,

until she opened her eyes and realized she just had masturbated, pleasuring herself to the thoughts of Juan.

Even though she was alone, she was feeling ignominious. She moaned and spoke out, and she knew that the running shower water could not cover her sexual sounds. A part of her smiled, and then she laughed, but that was short-lived when tears came down her face after realizing she needed love in her life. She needed someone to complete her. She wanted to feel loved, and at the same time reciprocate that love. She felt sad that Juan was the only one who seemed to notice her, without realizing the reason. Her job consumed her time and left her no chance to date or see men who were willing to date.

She was not too fond of the Internet with the Craigslist killer doing what he did, along with the other spurious individuals pretending to display affection with a motive. However, when it came to Juan, he made her feel special. His words seemed sincere. There was a promise of a good thing that was real when he spoke. It seemed strange to her, but when Juan spoke, a part of him was speaking the truth to and about Dawn. This is why his words connected with her, allowing her to visualize a better life, a love, and a brighter future filled with passion.

Dawn finished up in the bathroom and then made her way to check on Bree to see if she was okay.

When she came into the room, she sat beside her daughter, who was watching her cartoons.

"Bree, you okay in here, honey?"

"Yes, I'm watching Dora. I like this show."

"Well, Mommy is going to go watch TV in her room, okay?"

Breeana turned to Dawn and looked up at her mother with innocent eyes filled with curiosity.

"Mommy, who's Juan?"

Dawn was taken aback by the sudden question. She now realized how loud she was in the shower and felt a bit humiliated.

Who is Juan? she questioned herself before answering her daughter.

"Juan is a friend of Mommy's."

"When can I meet your friend, Mommy?"

"One day, honey. That's if you're a good girl," she added, placing the responsibility of Juan showing up on Bree.

She kissed Bree on the cheek before exiting the room and making her way to the bedroom to watch TV.

She jumped into the bed after arranging her pillows, pulling one close as if it were her man. She wished it could be Juan without the drama or risk of losing her job. She simply wanted them to be together living the good life.

The television was on, but her thoughts were taken over by images of Juan. She could not get him out of her head. He was the real thing, but was this opportunity worth the risk? It was a question she fumbled with for hours until she got out of the bed to retrieve a pen and writing pad.

Chapter 7

*T*he force of chemistry was working at its best. While Dawn was pouring out her thoughts and emotions, Juan was in his cell composing some poetry inspired by Dawn, not knowing if she would ever get the chance to read it. If she did, it would be a plus; if she did not, at least he expressed the thought.

Juan was coming to the conclusion that Dawn had all of the qualities Melanie obtained, just as Deja had, but in a different form. She was the best of the three. Maybe she was not the best looking of the three, but she was beautiful and sexy in her own way, which made her stand out overall.

The poem was titled "I Won't Forget." He flashed back and forth from the first conversation he had with Ms. O'Conner to the second conversation while glimpsing into the future and giving him more inspiration to compose the words of the poem.

I WON'T FORGET

If possible, I would like for this poem to open your eyes and mind to know things, kind of like setting yourself free of the past and taking time to reflect on you. Appreciate your worth and know that you are a queen—one of God's creatures. Your smile is one of your notable features, and your personality permeates through your smile, conversation, and your eyes. All of these things together display your patience.

As men, we forget to compliment your smile, your lips, your touch, your kiss, or that sweet scent—your signature—that allows us to know when you're near or in the room. It's a sweetness that enhances the mood.

I don't want to forget you or the things that made me gravitate toward you. I don't want to lose that flame when I look at you or when you're near. I want to feel that excitement, that fire igniting, that rush, and even that lust, because it makes falling for you fun.

I won't forget the things that made us—the laughter,

the love, the passion, and the trust. Sometimes, we forget the little things, but I won't forget the day you caught my eye or the day you started meaning more to me.

I won't forget how important your birthday is, because it's a day I celebrate you and a day I'll be your love slave. A day I want you to take advantage of me, even if this means I have to kiss and rub your feet. I know what it takes to keep you coming back to me.

I won't forget that with you I'm never alone. With that said, you should know that I'll never stay away from home.

I won't forget that with or without a ring. The commitment is in our hearts. So through the storm or darkest nights, I'll find my way back to you, because I won't forget where we started or that you're the one in my life where my heart is.

Written by Juan Dominguez
Inspired by someone special

After Juan finished the poem, he closed his notebook and felt better that he got out his thought. At the same time, a part of him was wishing that Ms. O'Conner accepted his proposal to have an open mind and open heart, so that she could one day be able to read and appreciate the words that were written specifically for her. Juan was in deep thought until he was interrupted by the security shakedown crew at his gate.

"Dominguez! Sanchez! Come to the gate and leave whatever is in your pockets in the cell. Only come out with your shower shoes and boxers shorts on," the security officer firmly voiced.

Juan mentally panicked while thinking about the letters from Melanie, the content of the letter from Deja, and the situation with Ms. O'Conner. So much was going on in his mind as he stripped down like he was told.

Puto was speaking Spanish to Juan about the guards wanting them to strip down to see their private parts.

They came to the cell gate once it was opened and stepped out.

"Face the wall. No talking to anyone else on the tier while we're in the cell. Don't move from the wall, or we'll take it as a threat or a breach of security. You understand what I'm saying to you?" the officer asked, showing a hint of his prejudiced side toward the Latinos.

"I understand, sir," Juan said before he then explained to Puto in Spanish.

All of the good thoughts he was having before they came into his cell disappeared, especially after being threatened not to move or talk.

The officers tore the cell apart. They flipped the mattresses; opened their record storage boxes; and dumped their soap, deodorant, toothpaste, and other cosmetics and commissary onto the bed, mixing both of their things together. It was more than a regular search. It was racism being displayed.

"Edward, look at this here!" the security officer said, after lusting at the pictures of Deja.

"That's definitely something to come home to. That's a nice piece of ass right there."

Juan couldn't handle standing there with his head facing the wall, so he leaned over to get a glimpse into the cell to see what they were looking at. It could have been a magazine or something, he thought, but he did not expect for it to be his personal photos of Deja.

Seeing this set him off. He was having thoughts of snapping on the racist officers, but it would interfere with what he had going on. He knew he would cross paths with them on the outside of the fences one day. Besides, saying something would only keep him in his cell longer and have the officers keep an eye on him closer. He did not want that type of recognition or attention. He just wanted them out of his cell. At the same time, he hoped they did not come across the letters that Melanie had written to him.

The one security officer flipped through the

mail in search of more personal photos and came across Melanie's letter; however, he did not pay any attention to the address or he would have stopped immediately.

"I think we're done here."

"Yeah, Edward! They'll have enough to clean up now. That's what they're good at anyway."

Juan could hear them speaking as if they were not in listening range. It angered him how disrespectful they were, showing their true colors while exploiting their positions to impose racism.

"Dominguez! Sanchez! Take it in. We're done here," the officer yelled out.

Juan and Puto stepped back into the cell. They were frustrated, and they felt compromised and violated in many ways, especially having the officers go through their personal effects.

"*Me no gusta policia,*" Puto said while picking up his things that were tossed about.

"Don't worry, Puto. Bad shit is going to happen to them. God does not like when people like that do bad to others. He keeps the balance."

Juan continued to converse with Puto while they cleaned up their cell to the way it was before the shakedown crew had arrived.

While they were finishing up cleaning, Dawn was at her place signing off on a letter she just had written to Juan, where she expressed her thoughts and emotions on the opportune occasion that was presenting itself.

She was trying to figure out if she should mail it out, or just allow that thought to be expressed on paper kind of like a diary. That was the million-dollar question of the day. She was once again struggling with her decisions and still not committing to the life she really wanted.

Chapter 8

At 12:32 p.m., Deja was out spending Juan's money; however, this time she could not blame her family. She was treating herself at the Harrisburg East Mall. She was at Lady Footlocker purchasing a pair of pink Air Jordans to match her tight, light blue Baby Phat jeans with pink trim and pink cat print. The shoes flowed with the pink T-shirt with the Baby Phat logo of the cat across the front.

The lifestyle she was accustomed to was the life Juan had lived when he was selling large quantities of cocaine. Now she was depleting the funds with no means of income other than her telemarketing job, which was the same job she called in sick from that morning to go shopping.

"Is there anything else I can help you with today, Deja?" the store rep asked, knowing Deja by name since she frequented the store a lot while spending Juan's money.

"I want those new Carmelos, but they don't have them in pink. You know that's my color."

"The baby blue still would look good on your feet," the salesperson replied, trying to sell the sneakers.

"Give them to me! You already know my size, but then I'll have to find something to wear with those."

It did not take long before the salesperson came out with the new Carmelos, and then rang up Deja at the register. It was almost $300 for just two pairs of sneakers. That did not include the three pairs of jeans in her other bag, along with the shirts and the Victoria's Secret lingerie and body sprays. The underwear was a surprise for Juan when he returned home in five months. She exited the store after paying in cash.

Deja then made her way over to King's

Jewelers to look for the perfect diamond earrings, and also to look at engagement rings. She still kept hopes of a happy ending for her and Juan, even though he would not be too happy to learn that she was still out spending his money.

She knew what she wanted as soon as she entered the store.

The clerk knew Deja came to spend, especially with the bags in her grasp that displayed she was on a shopping spree and having some me time.

"Can I help you with something today?"

"I'm looking for some good earrings to match with my outfit," Deja replied, lifting up her bags as if the sales rep could see inside.

As a female, she could relate to the shopping spree Deja was on. It was a girl thing.

"Do you have something in mind as in price range?"

"Just show them to me, and if I like them, I'll get 'em!"

The salesperson liked what she was hearing. It was money talk and a big commission for her.

"Take a look right here. We have a one-carat yellow diamond with great clarity."

"That is nice, but yellow though? I can only wear that with certain things."

"Okay, let's take a look at this one-carat white diamond. It has the three Cs: cut, clarity, and color."

"I like that. How much is that set?"

"It's $1,275 for the set, or $1,020 with our 20 percent discount."

"They're so small!" Deja responded after seeing that she could afford to buy something bigger.

"This is two and a half carats with the same quality as the one before. It's just a larger carat. The price tag $3,300."

"How much with the discount?"

"It would be $2,640," the salesperson quickly responded, already knowing the calculation on the merchandise.

"I'll take 'em!" Deja announced, setting down her bags to pull out $5,000 in $100 bills, folded just like Juan left them, all facing up.

The clerk knew Deja came to spend; however, she was not expecting to see her pull out a large sum of cash.

She placed the earrings in a black suede jewelry box and then rang her up.

"You made a good choice with the earrings. They'll look good on you," the salesperson said. She then added, "Will you be needing anything else?"

"No, but I am going to check out the engagement rings."

"If you like, you can even try on a few? You really get the getting-married effect when it's on your finger."

Deja loved the idea of trying on rings. It gave her hope. She was having a moment, flashing into the future, and seeing herself with Juan as he once promised. That promising future was before she did what she did, stealing his money, and now spending it as if he gave her permission.

Deja did not have any kids, but she wanted a boy and a little girl to make the perfect family. She wanted this and marriage before she was twenty-five years old. Now that she was twenty-one and just about to turn twenty-two, she wanted the life of which she dreamed.

"These rings are all so beautiful!" she said, feeling the love in her heart as her eyes became vitreous and formed tears of happiness.

A part of her knew what she was doing was wrong in spending his money, as if she had not done enough damage already financially and emotionally, after destroying the trust level and love they once had.

"Beautiful, yes, but not as beautiful as you are," a male voice came from behind.

She turned toward the voice and saw a dark-skinned, medium-built, model-like gentleman standing in a two-piece, white linen suit with a red alligator belt that matched his red gator shoes.

"Tears of happiness, which means I may have come into your life too late," he said smoothly and suavely as he flipped out his business card. "Tom Jones, president and CEO of Legacy Rentals."

"Thank you! Thank you for the compliment and the card."

"What's your name, beautiful?"

"Deja."

"Shouldn't your man be the one shopping for engagement rings, unless you're shopping for your special person," Tom said, referring to another female.

"I'm strictly dickly, papi! Nothing against chicks that like the kitty," Deja said, clearing that up, but thinking about the status of her and Juan. "My man is on a government vacation right now," she responded, referring to Juan's position as a government vacation.

Tom already knew he was in jail, because he lived that life already. Now he was living the affluent life since his business was doing well.

"So, he's not around. He's spending his time away from something so beautiful on lockdown. So, you're here living out your fantasy of getting married and having the good life, when the good life is right here waiting for you to take advantage of it."

Juan was good when it came to the wordplay, but Tom was even better, because he actually took the time to listen and observe, so that he would always know how and when to say and do things. He also had the advantage that he was thirty years old yet looked twenty-four or twenty-five and stayed in shape by living the good life.

Her tears of happiness were clear now. A smile formed on her face as thoughts slipped into her mind. Tom was making sense to her, but she could not just walk out on Juan again.

"I'm here because I was buying earrings. The engagement rings were a plus to look at," Deja responded, defending Juan's absence yet still appreciating the handsome model-like man before her. "I got your card," she added, wanting to end the conversation because of the timing.

"When your boy gets out, come down and rent a car for a week, and I'll give you a free weekend."

"Once again, papi, thank you for the card."

The salesclerk also appreciated Tom's look

after he flipped out another card and passed one over to her.

"Everybody has somewhere they need to go, and Legacy Rentals can help you get there."

The salesperson lit up inside, not knowing if he was coming on to her, or if the words flowing out of his mouth were just that soothing.

Tom turned away and walked over to the glass cabinet for a few seconds. Deja and the sales clerk both eyed him up and took in all his goodness.

Tom was conversing with another salesperson regarding a few pieces of jewelry he had seen in the case.

Minutes passed by, and just as Deja was preparing to leave, a male salesperson walked over to her.

"Excuse me, ma'am. The gentleman you were speaking with purchased this diamond bracelet for you. He said he hopes it goes well with your earrings."

The salesclerk slid the suede jewelry box across the glass countertop. Deja got the butterflies thinking about someone taking notice of her in the way that Tom did. It didn't happen too often. He did not resemble the normal type of guys she went after in the hood. He was someone you would see in a magazine or on a daytime soap opera. The way he spoke even made her feel as if she was in a scene from one of the shows.

"*Ahi Dios mio*, papi crazy! He spent like $5,000 on this!"

Deja was wrapped up in the money factor. She did not look at the quality of the diamond, the meaning behind the gift, or what it represented; however, in time, she would find out if she decided to call Tom. But why, when her heart and mind were supposed to be on Juan? Could she at least call to thank him? What would that lead to? She did not know what to think.

"Looks like you have no choice but to call him," the female salesclerk said, sounding almost envious that it was not her getting noticed or treated. "What can it hurt? Even if you go on a little date, it is the least you can do for something that special."

Deja clearly appreciated the diamond bracelet. It was something that would flow with the earrings.

"I guess I have a lot of thinking to do before I make the wrong decision and hurt someone either way."

Deja exited the store feeling good. She felt like a princess the way she spoiled herself and got spoiled by surprise.

Chapter 9

Juan quickly came out of his cell at 5:31 p.m. and made his way over to the phone before someone else got a chance to lock it down.

He needed to call Deja to see how she was doing and also to check up on his money. He knew that her hearing his voice would also make a difference versus the letter writing. It would add to her believing everything he said in the letters.

He wiped off the phone with his shirt, knowing how many people had been on it before him, and then he dialed the number after first putting in his inmate pin number.

The phone started ringing and ringing. He slipped into a thought of what he was going to say, just as her sexy voice came over the phone on the fourth ring.

"Hello."

The process of the phone call being accepted played out with the operator giving her the option to accept the call or hang up. She was excited knowing it was him on the other end, so she quickly pressed the 5 to accept the call.

"Hi, papi. I miss you so much!" she said with some sincerity. "*Que pasa, nena*? You being a good girl out there?"

"Why you ask that? You know I'm holding you down."

"It's been awhile since I've spoken to you or seen you, so I have to ask to make sure we're on the same page."

"Mmmmh, we on the same page, papi! I was thinking about coming to see you tomorrow. I got some new stuff I want to look good in for you."

Juan knew she always looked good with or without clothes on. The first thing that came to his mind was where the hell she was getting the money to buy new things.

"You got some new things, huh?"

"Si, papi, I did it for you," she responded in her sexy baby voice, trying to get her way.

"Deja, I forgive you for the past financial losses, but you can't keep burning my paper up like that."

He paused after hearing her smack her teeth, something she did when getting an attitude. He knew he could not afford for her to abort now. He needed to have control until he was able to retrieve his money from her. "Nena, we need to have something I can come home to, so we can live better and have the perfect ending to our love story. A love and a story we both have control over."

The phone call was briefly interrupted by the operator letting them know that the call was being recorded. The operator recording played three times per fifteen-minute call.

"I won't spend any more money, I promise. I have to hide it from myself," she said, being sarcastic and funny at the same time.

"I want you to send me $5,000, so my books can be secured."

Juan was thinking of at least having something to come home to in five months. He figured the worst-case scenario was that he could start back in the game with that amount if need be.

"Why you want so much, papi? I told you I wasn't going to spend your money," she responded, feeling the lack of trust in his tone and request.

"I'm thinking about us, nena. Besides, I want to make sure I don't want for anything while I'm here."

"Alright, I'll do it before I come see you tomorrow."

"Deja, I do love you," he said, wanting to remain on good terms before the call ended. "I need you in my life. I need your love, your good-good, your smile, and your Boricua attitude that makes you special."

She giggled hearing the words that made her feel good inside and out.

"I love you too, papi. Yo solo to quiero ati."

Juan could hear the change in her voice. She was in the moment, and he knew because it was something he heard in her voice before.

"I can't wait to see you tomorrow, so I can kiss them soft lips and hold your warm and soft body. I want you to feel the love racing from my body to yours."

Her heart fluttered feeling back in the place she once was with him—her comfort zone.

The thirty-second announcement came over the phone from the operator. They both got in a few more I love yous before the call came to an end.

Juan hung up the phone and made his way over to the table where Tre was playing tonk with his Crypt homies.

"Yo, what's up, Ike?" Tre addressed Juan.

"Ain't nothing, homie. Just got off of the jack with my little mami."

"You get that paper from her yet, or you going to let her take off on you again?"

Juan became silent, thinking about what Tre was saying. He was right. She was still spending his money, even though she gave her word not to continue running through his money.

Tre turned to his right where Juan was standing quietly in thought. He set down the cards to talk to his old cellmate.

"Talk to me, Ike. You know if she ain't doing too right, I can get it crackin' with my cuz out there?"

Juan was thinking about it, because she did

run away with $150,000, only to come back with $40,000+. Now she was back to spending it all over again. She was financially screwing him at the same time, and emotionally making him a cold-hearted individual. He lacked trust for anyone, which was why he always focused on manipulating those before him to get what he wanted.

"Check this out, amigo. I kill for $150,000. What you think I do for $150,000? I'm in a bad spot right now trying to maintain control over this punta."

"Say no more, Ike. You got this shit under control. My click of Crypts is on standby ready to ride for my Ike."

Juan respected Tre's gangsta and his willingness to ride out with him. He figured once he made it out to the other side, he would get Tre a good appeal lawyer to get him out or less time. He needed someone like Tre on his team.

"Everything is good, amigo. She's coming through tomorrow. I'll get inside of her head then. I'ma holla at you tomorrow, Tre," Juan said, taking it to his cell to lay back and think about the phone call he had with Deja as well as his conversation with Tre.

Chapter 10

Deja was laying out her new things at 7:31 p.m. at her place in Harrisburg for tomorrow's visit, when she came across Tom Jones's business card with his cell phone number on it. She set it to the side and then grabbed the earrings. She placed them with her new clothing and the gift box containing the diamond bracelet, which reminded her of Tom Jones.

She opened the jewelry box and exposed the flawless diamond with its carats sparkling, but not as much as the smile that parted on her face. Thoughts of the brief conversation she had with him crossed her mind, and his looks also helped absorb the memory of him.

She thought about calling him up simply to say thank you, but first, she needed to finish getting herself together for the visit with Juan.

She laid the card to the side while still smiling, before standing back to look at her outfit and make sure it was the way she wanted it. All the colors were flowing.

After approving the new clothing, she grabbed the cordless house phone and made her way into the bathroom, where she started running her bath water. She then poured lavender bubble bath into the water, which she had purchased from Victoria's Secret.

She dialed up Tom Jones's number as the hot water continued to run, crashing into the tub and forming bubbles as it mixed with the lavender soap.

"Talk to me!" Tom said when he answered his phone.

A brief second passed, and Deja was actually thinking about hanging up. She did not want to mess up with Juan, something she had already done, if only she knew. But this was only a thank-you, so what could it hurt?

"Hi, papi. It's me, Deja, from the mall."

"I'd be a fool to forget someone as rare and unique as yourself."

"I was just calling to thank you for the bracelet. It's so beautiful. I'll take good care of it."

"You're welcome, and the pleasure was all mine. I wish I could have stayed to see your smile when opening it, but business called." He then paused when hearing the bath water crashing into the tub. He visualized Deja with no clothes stepping into the tub and then out with water beads racing over her body. "If it's not too much to ask for, I would like to treat you to dinner!"

"I don't know, papi. I told you I'm kind of seeing someone. I just called to tell you thank you," she said, partially resisting some of the words that came out of her mouth.

Tom could hear the hesitation, along with the "kind of seeing someone" phrase, but it did not express promise or security.

"I was only looking for a reason to see you in the flesh wearing the bracelet; besides, you're *kind of* seeing someone, which means you're doubting something about this someone."

The water turned off, and then her hand parted the water to check if it was to her liking. She then slipped out of her clothes with the phone still in hand and stepped in one foot at a time as she adapted to the hot soothing water.

Tom was visualizing her once more after hearing her speak as she went through the process.

"Mmmh, this water is hot, but it feels good," she said, stretching the word good almost seductively. "Hold on, papi, let me get situated," she said, sliding down into the lavender bubble bath that had engulfed her body. "I needed this! I had a long day, you know?"

"I can imagine, with shopping."

Tom was imagining himself being there with Deja, speaking with her as she relaxed in the tub, while adding his soothing words of truth and promise to her.

"One date, papi! That's the least I can do to show you my appreciation for getting me this nice bracelet."

"The bracelet was a gift, no strings attached, or obligations needed. I want you to come on this date because something inside you wants to get to know more about me—and more importantly, because you really want to go on the date."

Her heart felt a tingle. Was it his words reaching deep that had some meaning and truth? Whatever it was, it brought another smile to her face and heart. No compunction, for this was innocent.

"I'll come because I want to come, so you better be good to me when I get there."

Tom was enjoying the conversation. There was a little foreplay on the mind, trying to figure out what was needed to appease her in every way.

"Good is the only way I know how to treat a lady."

She loved hearing his voice. It was stimulating, pleasing, and soothing.

"Besides, if you weren't what I thought of you, then I would have never given you a second look or the bracelet. There was something about you that stood out. You are shining and radiant, yes, but in a different light; but then again, I could need a checkup to see if my eyes are deceiving me," he joked, getting her to giggle and moan as if his words were fingers stroking her pleasure spot.

She did not want the call to end now. Somehow his words turned her on, and she found herself stroking her love spot. A sensation soared through her body as she imagined seeing his face close to her as he continued to speak. She was caught in the moment. It had been seven months without the real thing, so her imagination was all she had until now. It was his voice, the visions of him at the mall, and the way he addressed her. He was everything a woman could want.

Her fingers disappeared in and out as they slid along her clitoris. Her eyes remained closed while she licked her lips with a smile.

"Thank you, papi."

She hesitated while feeling the buildup of the sensation that she wanted to be released the more her fingers worked their magic.

"I hope you are a good man, so at least having me come on this date will be worth my time."

"Trust me, if you don't leave with a smile and a full stomach, I promise never to bother you again."

He was sounding like he was ready to end the call, but she did not want him to hang up. She was still in her special place caressing her love spot and trying to reach her point of eruption with him in mind.

"You sound like you're trying to hang up. Mmmh, mmmh! Hold on, papi!" she spoke and moaned while feeling the release.

He knew what she was doing. In fact, he thought it was unique and sexy. It made him want her even more.

"I think after the date, you'll be the luckiest woman in the world, or at least that's how I plan to make you feel," he said before he became quiet upon hearing her panting as the heavy flow rushed through her body and escaped as her fingers slid in and out.

She bit down on her lip, with her eyes still closed with images of Tom's fingers instead of hers working the magic just as his words were filled with something special.

"Damn, papi!" she said in a distant low sexual whisper, reaching the end of her passionate climax.

Her eyes remained closed, since she did not want to ruin the moment.

"So, when are we going on this date and where?" she said breaking his silence, knowing he heard her.

But she displayed no shame or embarrassment. It was a female thing that men should view as a privilege if they ever get the opportunity to experience such a thing.

"I was thinking about tomorrow late dinner—maybe around 7:30 p.m. As for the place, how about Warren Charles, which overlooks the Susquehanna River?"

Warren Charles was a five-star restaurant located on the west shore with a great view of the downtown Harrisburg, along with the lighted bridges connecting each shore.

"I'll see you then, papi. Thanks again for the bracelet and answering my call," she said, feeling good after pleasuring herself.

"You're more than welcome. Take care, beautiful, and I'll see you at dinner."

After they hung up, she put her head back on the plastic tub pillow and relaxed as she thought about the call. She then wondered how the hell she allowed herself to go that far, when a part of her heart was with Juan.

Chapter 11

*D*awn was just pulling in to work at 7:45 a.m. She really did not want to be there to work, but she was motivated to see Juan. He also needed to figure out how she was going to help him out, since he was not exactly on her caseload. She needed to have another face-to-face with him, something that would assure her that he was who he said he was, and not just because he was in a vulnerable position in search of affection. She wanted confirmation, so she could open up to him and express herself to him as she did in the letters—the same letters she was holding until she was sure about him.

Her plan was coming together as she made her way to the main entrance. She then pulled out her work ID as she entered the building.

"Good morning, Ms. O'Conner," the officer

said.

"Good morning, Officer McClain," she responded, before swiping her ID and then punching in her secured number.

She made her way into her office and closed the door behind her. She needed privacy, knowing she would not have much of that once the new commits started to flow in.

"What are you getting yourself into, Dawn?" she questioned herself as she reached for the phone to call the H-block sergeant.

"H-block Sergeant Stern speaking."

Sergeant Stern was a thorough Afro-American brother. He also used to be a fighter, something he displayed when it came time to rough up a few inmates or just show off to the inmates with whom he was cool.

"Sergeant Stern, this is Dawn O'Conner over here at reception."

"How can I be of assistance, Ms. O'Conner?"

"I'm looking for a Juan Dominguez. We need to get his paperwork squared away, since there was a slight problem."

She was lying, but it was the only thing she could think of to get him over to reception in her office without making it obvious.

"You need him now?" Sergeant Stern asked, looking at his watch to see what time it was. "I got the guys taking showers. As soon as we're done here, I'll send him over."

"Thank you, sergeant."

She hung up and thought about her man in the shower—her shower that is, not the jailhouse shower. She wanted to be in the closed shower with steam filling up the bathroom, bodies close together, and his hands massaging her shoulders down to her lower back while releasing the tension of the day. They would make small conversation about the day. It would be a real life with a real man giving her real love.

Her imagination was interrupted by a knock at her office door followed by the intake captain walking inside. He handed her a list with all the names of the new inmates arriving as well as their charges and sentences.

"Good morning, Dawn. We have about fifty-five guys coming through today from Dauphin, Cumberland, and York Counties."

"So it's going to be a busy day? Make sure your guys roll 'em in and out."

"They know the drill. No dicking around. Excuse my language, but I have to stay on top of these guys. Some of them are only working here because of their family members in high places," the captain said as he exited and closed the door behind him.

Dawn looked over the paper and established the files so when they came in, she would just ask a few questions, fill in the blanks, and get them out of her office.

~ ~ ~

Juan was standing in front of reception at 8:15 a.m. with a pass in his hand. He had been escorted by a corrections officer since reception was close to the exit of the front gate. Juan did not have a low clearance code of 2mv, 2mc, or lc, which were codes that would allow him to go outside the gate without the escort of a corrections staff member.

"What you need?" the officer came over the intercom after the button to enter was pressed by the other officer.

"I got one coming to see Ms. O'Conner to get his records straight."

"All right, I'll buzz you all the way through," the officer in the control center said while looking at the monitor at his fellow officer and Juan.

The two doors to enter the control reception area that led to Dawn's office were buzzed, which allowed them to walk through.

The officer walked Juan over to the office before knocking on the door and sticking his head inside.

"Dominguez is here. You called for him off of H-block?"

"Yes, thank you, Officer. Mr. Dominguez, come in and have a seat."

The officer walked away to converse with his buddies while Dawn was excited to see Juan all fresh and clean.

"Good morning, Mr. Dominguez, I see we have a problem with your file," she said, still hanging her head down while looking at the bogus file that was supposed to be his.

It was her way of breaking the ice, so to speak, and also to give the officer enough time to get away from her office.

On the other hand, Juan immediately thought about his sentence being corrected. His heart pounded in fear, yet his face remained calm. His mind raced with thoughts of his next out, because doing time was not for him.

His silence caused her to lift her head and make eye contact with him. Her eyes said it all. They were happy; and right then, he knew she was messing with him.

"Good morning, Ms. O'Conner."

"That it is, and now that you're here," she began with a smile, "I needed to see you." She felt like it was a teenage crush.

Her voice almost sounded desperate. It was not bad, but good, which allowed Juan to realize that she was now serious about what he was actually saying to her.

"I've been doing some thinking—thoughts of you, our conversation, and your words. Is this real? I mean, is what you want from me something real, or is it just to pass time while you're here?"

Juan adjusted himself in the chair and made eye contact. He could feel the chemistry, the moment, and the emotions of something real and something right.

"Every word that comes out of my mouth when I speak to you is meant for you. It's meant to connect with you and your heart on a mature level."

Once again, he was charming his way into her heart while appeasing her mind and securing a place in her life.

"I'm going to open up to you. I just hope that you don't break my heart, or I don't lose my job in the process of falling for you. I see that you're a genuine person that found yourself in a bad position. I know that once you're out of here, we can really have something special, if you don't leave me when you walk out of these doors."

She was testing him to see his reaction with her ending statement.

"Why walk out of a movie when the story is just getting good, or get up from the table before I'm done eating? I believe you have plenty to offer not just me, but our relationship. That's if you don't mind me saying *ours* as in me and you?"

She shook her head with a smile almost as if she could not believe what she was hearing, or what she was doing in the office at her work conversing with an inmate about a relationship.

"*Us* sounds good."

"I wrote a poem the other day. Actually, you inspired the words to it. It's titled 'I Won't Forget.' When we establish communication, I'll share it with you, so you know what I was thinking at that moment."

"I have a confession to make too. I've been writing letters to you. I've been trying to figure out what to say and how to say things to you, and also expressing how emotional I can be. Because when I come into a relationship, I give my all with hopes of getting the same in return."

"Like I said, when we establish communication, we can share our thoughts and emotions, and tell each other how our day went. Therefore, if you don't get a chance to see me, it's not a day missed."

His words were almost poetic and rhythmic, just like music to her ears and heart.

She was smiling from ear to ear, which was something not only Juan noticed, but Melanie caught as she walked by Dawn's office. From a female standpoint, her instincts kicked in. She knew that Juan was probably flirting with Dawn or complimenting her, and a slight hint of jealousy came over Melanie until she reminded herself of the money. With her, it was all about business.

Dawn was unaware of Melanie walking by, since she was caught up in Juan's words and physical presence.

"I'll send you a letter out tonight when I get home. Make sure when you get my mail to always tear off the return address. I don't want it to get in the wrong hands. Remember, I have a baby girl at home that depends on me."

She trusted Juan, and he appreciated this. It was a step toward something rewarding—the perfect love story. He was beginning to really see himself with her outside of jail. She was the real thing.

"You can and will always be able to trust me. I believe in karma, because it has a way of keeping the balance."

"God keeps the balance. He also places people in your life for a reason, which is why I believe that this is meant to be. Just don't prove me wrong."

"Stop saying that!" Juan said, leaning forward before pausing to look over his shoulder. He then reached his hand across the desk and touched hers, which sent a warm sensation rushing through her body to her heart. "I'm going to be good to you and for you now, and even more when I get there. As for your baby girl . . ." He paused, not knowing her name until he saw a photo of her with her name and school drawings underneath. ". . . Breeana. I plan on making both of you the happiest women in the world. If you talk, I'll listen. After a long day at work, I'ma massage your feet, kiss you where it aches the most, and release the tension in your body. I may even cook a good meal for you, since I know how to work my way around in the kitchen a little."

All the visions she had of him were right. He was saying he would do these things she thought he would do. This could not be wrong, because it was feeling so right.

His hand on top of hers added to the

affection that she was feeling.

"As much as I would like to call you to my office once a day or once a week, it's going to be hard to do because of where I'm located. So, I have to come up with something so I can at least see you once a week, and see how my man is doing."

"Whatever you do, be smart about it, because I want you to keep your job. I'll always be here for you no matter what. We'll figure something out."

He puckered his lips and simulated a kiss before he slowly pulled back and leaned in his chair.

In her mind, the kiss was as real as it gets. It was the closest she had been kissed in so long. His hand on hers made it even more special. The fact that she was doing something with someone she was not supposed to be doing it with added to the intrigue. Their moment was abruptly interrupted when the reception captain knocked on the door and then stuck in his head.

"We got a bus unloading now. Just giving you a heads-up to make sure we're rolling."

"Thank you, Captain Wakefield," she said with a serious business look, erasing the passion-filled smile from her face.

"Now that we had this little talk, big things and better days are to come next," Juan said, knowing the conversation was coming to an end.

"You keep your promise to be good to me, and I'll promise to be the best woman you ever had."

For once, Juan was taken by her words. This was it. It was something special, something real, and something he was now looking forward to building on once he was released.

"Well, Mr. Dominguez, I'll sign your pass, and you can head back to your block to do whatever it is you guys do over there," she joked.

"I'll be writing out my thoughts and emotions on paper with hopes of connecting with someone special."

"Sounds good, and let's hope it's as good as it sounds," she said playfully with a smile.

Juan did not come back. He knew she was now his. He also knew he was going to treat her differently than any other woman he ever had. Without question, she was different. She was wife material.

Chapter 12

Juan was in his cell at 1:23 p.m. still waiting to be called for a visit from Deja. He was beginning to think she was not going to come. Visiting hours were from 8:30 a.m. to 4:00 p.m. except for Thursdays, when the visiting room was open from 1:00 p.m. to 8:00 p.m., which allowed those who worked first shift to have a visit.

Juan smelled good wearing the Blue Nile oil he purchased from one of the Muslims in the yard. He mixed the oil in with his lotion to add scent and make it last longer.

"Dominguez, you in there?" a voice came across the intercom in the cell.

The rest of the inmates were in the yard, school, or at work.

"Yeah, I'm here," he replied, knowing it

should be his visit.

"You have a visit, so come on out."

He exited the cell, but not before checking himself out one more time in the mirror.

He secured the pass from the guard before he made his way toward the visiting room.

As he approached the crosswalk, which was another secured section where an officer checked inmate passes, he noticed Melanie coming out of the officer's dining room.

He handed his pass to the officer to check. He at least wanted to catch her before she made it past him, but the officer was looking at his pass and checking the time, location, and destination.

"Alright, enjoy your visit," the officer said before he handed him the pass back.

Juan took long strides trying to make up for the seconds wasted with the officer checking his pass.

Melanie did not notice him at first. She was more focused on unwrapping the Pop-Tart she just had purchased from the vending machine.

A part of him was excited to see her, since he wanted to keep her in position and on his side.

Less than twenty yards away now, she looked up and placed a piece of the Pop-Tart into her mouth to savor the flavor. Her eyes turned to the fast-moving inmate approaching from the other direction, only to see that it was Juan. She wanted to give him a serious look, especially after spotting him in Ms. O'Conner's office that morning, but she could not resist the smile that came across her face. She remembered the money he had given her and, more important, the letter he sent letting her know she was his type.

Neither of them spoke to the other. Instead, they simply passed by each other, which was enough for the both of them. They knew they could not afford to be compromised or noticed by anyone seeing them fraternizing.

His brief smirk was enough for her. She was back on track, erasing what she thought she had seen that morning.

As for him, he took notice of how she stepped up her wardrobe with the money he had given her. Her hair and nails were done, and her French manicure allowed the half-carat tennis bracelet to stand out.

He stopped to allow her to pass by like a zephyr. Being a gentleman, he also wanted to get a glimpse of her as a gentle breeze of her new fragrance trailed behind her. It was Kim Kardashian's new fragrance, Dashing, which was sweet, aromatic, and memorable, and it made him want to follow her just to be close and passionate.

He was quick in taking a glimpse, knowing the rules at the prison. Reckless eyeballing was considered misconduct if a prisoner stared at a female employee too long.

Juan entered the main building and showed his pass to the second checkpoint officer in the control bubble, so he could get through the next set of gates.

After making it down to and through the strip-down area, Juan headed out to his visit after giving the office his pass and taking a seat to wait for Deja to enter.

"Dominguez, your visit is here."

He stood from the chair and finally saw Deja face-to-face. She was glowing and seeing her took him back to when it was all love and everything was all good. Her curves showed through the tight jeans, with her shirt pressing against her perky full breasts. The diamond studs were sparkling, and her hair was pulled back around to lie over her right shoulder and close to her breast. Her lips were not just looking soft, but glossy from the lip balm. He took a few steps to greet her, instinctively pulling her close and erasing every bad thing about her at that moment as their lips connected and osculated with passion. His hands started to slide down her back before he remembered the visiting rules.

"I miss your soft lips, papi," she said in a low sexy voice.

"I miss all of this!" he responded, speaking the truth for once, which was something she managed to bring out of him when they were face-to-face.

There was something from their long relationship that neither of them could deny.

They made it to their seats among the other visitors in the room. Some kids played with other kids while the mothers interacted with the kids' fathers. All the inmates snuck kisses and touches, and some of them received packages.

Juan was doing a little bit of kissing and touching, something he really had not done other than touching Ms. O'Conner's hand. He was snuggled up with Deja with his arm around her and his lips on her neck every time the guard was not looking.

"Damn, I miss you, mami. I wish I could make love to you right now!"

"Stop, before you start something you can't finish!" she said, getting turned on by his closeness, gentle touch, and words.

"Alright, get up and get me a soda and some of them chicken wings—like two packs."

"How many wings you want?" she asked as she grabbed her plastic bag full of quarters.

"You wasn't listening. Where's your mind at? I said two and a Coke."

Her mind was on the date with Tom, which was the same reason why she showed up late. She pleasured herself once more the previous night before going to bed. And to add to her fantasy, she dreamt of Tom, so she slept in.

It was so wrong, but felt so right; besides, it was only a dream. It was only masturbation and not the real thing.

Juan watched Deja's ass as she walked away to the machine, and he flashed back to when it was good between the two of them. The first kiss. The first time he made love to her. All the good, only to be betrayed by her, for what? Money? The root to all evil. Damn, mami! he thought, wondering why she gave up all they had just for money. He was struggling with seeing her, and now having this new thing with Dawn. He figured he would just play things out. Money was not more important than love, but it was the trust and betrayal factor that weighed on him the most.

As Deja was coming back with the food, he took a real good look at her. He appreciated all of her beauty, style, and smile accented by the mole above her lip. He also took notice of the sparkling diamond bracelet, and dollar signs went off in his mind. He knew how much something like that would cost if it was real, and he knew it would be the first question he would ask her.

"Here you go, papi. I know you miss my good cooking."

"I miss more than your good cooking," he said after giving her ass a light slap and feeling the softness.

"I told you, you better stop, before you start something you can't finish."

"We can go in the bathroom or right here. I don't care if people watch. It'll make it more exciting!" Juan joked, knowing he would not do her like that.

"Damn, that sounds like some real freaky shit, papi!"

Juan dug into the chicken wings and chased it down with the Coke. He was now ready to address the spending issue as well as the bracelet.

"I can't lie, mami. You do look amazing; and more important, I appreciate you coming to visit. But let's talk about the serious stuff. You know, the things that will help us build or rebuild the damage that's been done."

"What do you mean, papi?" she asked, almost in a stressed voice, wondering what just had happened to the lovey-dovey stuff.

"I'm talking about the money situation you were doing when I came to jail. That shit hurt me, not only financially but emotionally. I trusted you and only you with everything," Juan said while still using a calm tone. He knew that his message would still be received. "Deja, I can't deny the way we are when we're together. The chemistry is fun, exciting, and explosive."

She loved those words. "But we can't ignore what has happened without seriously addressing the trust issue, just like I can't ignore that expensive-looking set of earrings or bracelet."

"The earrings were cheap, and the bracelet was a gift."

She was so quick to respond that she did not even realize what she said would start another problem.

"A gift!" His voice raised slightly, knowing guys buy girls gifts like that with only one thing on their mind: getting some of the goods. "You got people buying you gifts?"

"*Tranquillo*, papi! I don't have no one doing anything. This *moreno* got it for me when I was getting these," she explained as she pointed to her earrings.

Juan knew it would not be long before she slipped away for good. He could not compete with someone that was actually there for her compared to him being in jail. Five months remaining did not mean anything, and even if Deja knew, which she did not, she still was under the pretense that he was going to be sitting for some time.

"I'm not even going to trip. Just make sure you put your spending on pause. I need my paper for when I come home."

She reached her hand behind his neck and caressed him to show affection. He was her first true love. She knew she messed up, not just with the money but with accepting Tom Jones's gift.

"I'm sorry, papi. You know I love you. You don't understand how it is for me out there without you. You were my everything, and then all of a sudden, you were gone just like that sitting on this time. That shit be killing me inside."

He was facing forward as her fingers

caressed the back of his neck. A woman's touch was special, and her words were even more heartfelt, but how much of it was deception? He knew she always wanted things her way, and she also knew how to bring calm to any situation to make him happy. He turned to her and made eye contact. He felt what little love remained in their tortuous relationship.

"Dame un beso, nena."

She leaned in to kiss his lips while her fingers still caressed his neck, sending the passion with ease. She was working him, although her intentions might not have directly been as such. But entertaining the date with Tom Jones was something Juan did not know about nor would he approve of.

Juan pulled back from the kiss just in time to see Melanie staring back at him.

She came into the visiting room pretending to use the vending machine, knowing Juan had come to a visit, because she had checked the computer and saw when the visitor logged in as well as who the visitor was, Deja. The same person he told her was just an ex handling his money.

Her face was balled up and her eyes became glassy. She was feeling tricked.

Juan could not say anything, nor could she. He needed to think of something quick, so he jumped up.

"I got to use the bathroom," he said to Deja, excusing himself and making his way over to the desk.

The inmate bathroom was separate from the visitors' bathroom. He had to go through the same hallway that Melanie came through to get to the bathroom, which provided him the perfect opportunity to explain himself, if he could.

He arrived at the desk to retrieve the inmate

bathroom pass before making his way into the hallway. Melanie came up behind him shortly thereafter.

"What the fuck was that?" she questioned, trying to contain her tone; however, her emotions took over. "You told me she was just an ex taking care of things!"

"You saw that I kissed her, but you didn't see me resisting the whole visit. She has my money, and she's trying to use me as long as she has it. It's what she calls leverage," Juan explained, thinking fast on his feet.

She could not refute what he said, because it was plausible.

"You said good things in your letter to me, and I was willing to believe you. I am a good girl, you know?"

He could not believe this was happening. He needed to have Melanie in good spirits and on good terms. He also needed to get out of the hallway because he only had a certain amount of time before the officer called him back to the dressing area to see what was taking so long.

He scanned over her shoulder and then over his own. There were no cameras in the hallway, so he pulled Melanie close and briefly hugged her before he placed a kiss on her neck. He felt the passion of his warm lips on her neck, which sent a vibe of affection to her heart and confirmation that he was not lying. His lips then moved quickly to her lips, which was something she did not resist. It was quick but passionate.

Her eyes were now filled with happiness as he managed to pull it off once more. The strange thing was that the brief kiss made him want more, but not from Deja, since he knew what that was like. It did not have that special feeling anymore, but that brief kiss was unique in itself, and Melanie felt the same.

"I'll write you tonight, plus I'll get her to send

you some more money, okay?"

"Thanks, and, yes, now I'm okay."

"We got to get out of here before I get in trouble kissing them soft lips."

She smiled as his words sent a tingling sensation to her heart, which made her eyes sparkle.

"Bye, amigo."

She did not even care about the money at that point. She believed what he was saying in his letter. The money just happened to be a plus.

Juan made his way back into the visiting room and over to Deja, who was gathering her things and getting ready to leave.

"Damn, mami, you ready to roll on me?"

"I forgot my mom needed me to take her somewhere. My aunt was supposed to, but she went to AC to gamble with her friends at work."

She was lying. She wanted to leave so she could pick out something nice to wear for her date with Tom Jones later that night.

"Alright, whenever you can, make sure you come through. It's always a pleasure and a privilege to see you and that fat ass!" Juan said, embracing her before kissing her on the cheek and then the corner of her lips. "Oh, take five more over to that spot. After you handle that, I'll let you know when I come home. You better be ready for that too. It's sooner than you think!" he announced while eyeing her down and then hugging her to leave.

Juan now had his hands full. Dawn was serious, and Melanie was full of jealousy, displaying signs of a serious yet potentially problematic situation. As for Deja, she wanted to be in control of the destiny of her emotions, which meant if it was going to be over, it was going to be on her terms, not his. Juan had a lot to handle in this truly unwieldy situation.

Juan headed back to the block to absorb the

day he'd had thus far, after seeing Dawn, Melanie, and Deja all in the same day. Melanie was back in reception conversing with Dawn, something that was out of the norm, but she was securing her interest, remembering that Juan was in her office that morning.

"I see you started the day off busy with that Puerto Rican guy. He gets around. He must be someone important, like Mr. Dupont. I saw him on the crosswalk and then on a visit with a real pretty Latina."

Dawn looked up from her paperwork, wondering why Melanie was in her office sharing this information. It was not normal and plucking Juan out as she did was also not normal.

"You said Puerto Rican. Now if you take a look at this list right here, there are at least twenty that came in today, so which one of them are you speaking about in particular?" Dawn questioned, knowing what she was doing.

Melanie's eyebrows angled a little, not realizing her reverse psychology did not play out on Dawn, being a counselor.

"Never mind! How's your day so far?"

"It would be better if I could get this work done!" Dawn sarcastically responded, hinting she wanted her out of her office.

Melanie stood up after realizing that Dawn was being smart about her response as well as about acting as if she did not know who she was talking about. Dawn had to protect her best interest, which was her and her baby girl, which meant she needed to keep her job to do so.

As soon as Melanie exited the office, Dawn turned to her computer. Her fingers danced across the keys as she punched in Juan's information to see who came to visit him and how long she had stayed. She was taken aback to see that he actually did have a visitor come to see him. Now she needed to know who the female was before she fell for the wrong one.

Dawn also knew there was a reason behind Melanie's motive for coming into her office and dropping the information on her like she did. She just could not or did not want to visualize Juan with her. Those images of Juan were for her only, or so she thought.

y 6:07 p.m., Juan was in his cell writing letters to Deja, Melanie, and Dawn to recap the day with each of them, and also to make sure all the pieces were where they needed to be with each of the women. He was truly serious about Dawn. Deja had a piece of his heart from the past; however, she was also the same person that betrayed him. As for Melanie, something about her was growing on him, even though it started off as all business.

Deja:

Today's visit was kind of crazy with mixed emotions. A part of me was loving to see you, and it took me back. Like I said, I can't lie, but you know we have to work on us. That's if you want what I want? It's a question you have to answer, or should I say a question your heart has to answer. Just know that when the money is gone, love will still be here. Love can't be spent; however, it can be wasted if it's not appreciated. I'm not going to burn you out with what you already know you should be doing. Just keep your heart and mind right, and we'll be on the same page. Take care of yourself, mami.

P.S. Don't forget to take care of shorty with that money. Love Juan/Tu amor

After he was done writing the letter, he turned his attention to his 19-inch color flat-screen. He saw that the six 'o clock news was showing a major drug bust that took place in Harrisburg and Philadelphia. What really caught his attention, once he zoomed in, were the faces of his cocaine connections and people he dealt with before catching his charge. He turned up the volume to hear what the reporter was saying.

"Raphael Gomez and Orlando Mantalvo, two drug lords out of Juarez, Mexico, were distributing tons of cocaine in the Pennsylvania area. FBI sources state they've been onto these men for some time, hoping that this brings a halt to the flow of cocaine into this country. Although, they doubt this ever since the notable and pernicious drug cartel boss, Donna Tulia, took over, displaying violence to anyone not siding with her organization, including authority figures. President Obama is in talks with the Mexican president to see what they can do to halt the flow of drugs into this country, as well as the murders of those in association believed to be in cooperation with the federal authorities."

Juan could not believe what he was seeing with the skids of cocaine and the large sums of money. He knew his Mexican friends were connected, but not like that.

He turned the TV back down, so he could get back to his letters. Melanie was next.

Hola mami/Mel B:

The kiss. I have to start off with that since it was everlasting. Although brief, the impression on my mind is still there lingering just as your sweet scent, which was something I caught when kissing your neck. I hope you like that too! I didn't want you to be mad. It's not how I want to continue on with you, whether it be for money, or you and I making something special come up out of this. Keep in mind that originally you came at me for 150 stacks. Truth be told, if I made you my girl, or if we made this 100 percent official, you could have the world. Besides, I know in a real relationship, money is good, but love lasts longer.

Mel, I felt something today. I didn't know that your presence or closeness would bring that out of me, but it did. I wish we had more alone time, but the closest we'll get to that, until I come home, are my words and your words connecting. They will be the hands that reach out to comfort one another.

Mel, when I think about what took place today, I don't ever want you to be sad or mad because of me. I want you to always know me by and for good things. Kind of like that vibe you felt when I saw you pass by.

Words didn't need to be exchanged. Just seeing you smile as you did meant enough to me as did seeing that you put the money to good use. You was looking good, mami. Like I said, I need more time with you, but right now your letters and true commitment will do.

When I get there, we're going to do something special. Maybe take a little vacation so I can spoil you a little while being your love slave at the same time. I know you can get used to that? I need you to believe that you deserve a good thing, that being me. What I can offer you mentally, emotionally, financially, and physically is to give you that comfort and affection to make you feel special inside and out. If you open up your heart and mind to believe this, then where we can go from here is limitless. Mel, I'm going to close on that note, giving you something to think about and something to hold on to. Take care.

Sincerely,
Your secret associate/amor to be

Juan took a break from writing and got up to stretch out before going into his letter with Dawn. He made some juice, opened a bag of

Middlesworth bar-b-cue chips, and munched a little while processing his day. He also thought about what he was going to say to Dawn. He knew his words were not going to be game.

The letter to Deja was short and to the point, although filled with some game. A part of him held on to what used to be a good thing; the other part of him knew it would never be as it was again.

Melanie's letter was 70 percent truth and 30 percent game. He really did feel something when he kissed her. She really did have all the good qualities of a girlfriend; however, when it came to Dawn, she was wife material.

He brushed the chip crumbs from the writing paper before he started on his third letter.

Dear Dawn:

I sat back thinking about our face-to-face conversation and the risk you took calling me into your office. That in itself displays sacrifice, something a relationship is all about. Since we are official, as your man, I now hold you high in a very special place—that place being in my heart and on my mind. Having such status means I'm going to put you first, pay attention, and give you the much-needed time. This specific element in itself will give you what is needed to grow into a good thing, a good love. That's simply me always being good to you.

Dawn, with you in my life, I'll do the right thing, live on the right path, and not sell drugs, because I don't want you and me to invest emotionally and mentally into this relationship, only for me to be taken away or sent to jail. I'll get a job, finish my degree, and put it to use. I'm looking forward to being with you and Breeana, and being the father figure she needs. So, I guess since I don't have any kids, she'll be my first princess?

I'm glad we're taking advantage of this opportunity. It's fate! This was meant to be. I feel it in my heart, and it's feeling good right now. Well, beautiful, I'm going to bring this letter to a close. I hope you like the poem I'm putting in here too. It's the one I was telling you about. Take care.

Respectfully,
Juan

Juan did not have Dawn's address yet. He was waiting on her to send her letter first, and then he would send it off. But he needed to get the thought out while he was feeling in the mood.

~ ~ ~

Dawn was at her place expressing her thoughts and emotions on paper, in between flashing to the moment in the office when Juan touched her hand. It was the second time he had done this, and each time she felt something special. Now with their emotions and thoughts out in the open, it made his touch even more unique. His touch was something she was looking forward to every day, once he was home staying with her, or at least this was how she planned it.

Breeana was in her bedroom watching television in between playing with her toys.

Dawn placed her letters in a large envelope. She also added a picture of Breeana to go along with the heartfelt letter she wrote, hoping that her message would be poignant enough to secure her interest in the relationship.

She lay back on her bed and grabbed the pillows from the other side, the place Juan would sleep once he came home.

The thought alone made her smile and feel good as she hugged the pillow.

She closed her eyes and found herself in a place of fantasy. It was a place that made her feel warm and comforted by Juan's presence. He was in her visions next to her lying on the bed beside her, looking into her eyes while caressing her hair. His fingertips lightly glided across her hairline and down to her ear. She loved his touch. It was so gentle and passionate. Although she could not hear him, she read his lips as the words formed, "I love you and I'll always take care of you." She was in a place far past the stage that they were in their relationship. She was months or years into the future in her fantasy.

After reading his lips, they came close to hers. It was so right as if it was the first kiss. It was special. His hands and fingers still caressed her hair as their lips interlocked passionately and a light moan came out. But this was the love racing through her body. Her heart was pounding in satisfaction. His hands slipped down her side and around to her soft ass. She loved the way his touch felt, and she wanted to be closer. She was deep into her imagination and her fantasy world of her and Juan. She did not hear the doorbell ring, but she did hear Breeana yell out to her.

"Mommy! Mommy! Somebody's at the door!"

Breeana was standing on the other side of the bed facing her mother, who was somewhat smiling, halfway stuck in her fantasy world.

"What are you smiling for, Mommy?"

"Nothing, Bree! Come on, let's see who's at the door."

Dawn was already in her red cotton pajamas from Walmart. They made her comfortable, and that was all that mattered.

She looked through the peephole when she got to the door and saw someone she had not seen in years. It was her ex-fiancé. The last time she saw him was almost a year after Breeana was born. He broke off their engagement after he was caught cheating. He ended up marrying the other girl. Johnny Catillino left Pennsylvania when the US Marines shipped out to go overseas. He was a private then.

Dawn did not know what to think or if she wanted Breeana even to see him.

"Bree, go have a seat on the couch real quick."

"Why? I want to see who's at the door."

"Because I said so, Bree. Now let Mommy take care of this please."

Bree turned with a sad face after not getting her way. She did not understand that it was grown-up business that needed to be handled.

She opened the door, and he turned around. Emotions arose. They were mixed emotions. He still looked good standing there in his Marines uniform. He was of Italian background and stood five foot eleven and weighed a fit 190 pounds. He had a bald head and clean-shaven face. Although he was thirty-two, he could easily pass for twenty-four since he stayed in such good shape.

"What are you doing here?" Her voice was

somewhat strained yet filled with anger and pain.

"I came to see my daughter," he responded, raising the half-dozen flowers with a Dora doll in the other hand. "I'm sorry for everything. I even apologize for the emotions you feel toward me right now."

"You didn't just leave me! You left her!" Dawn said, trying not to raise her voice. "She doesn't even know who you are other than the old pictures I have of you."

"Can you at least let me see her to give her this gift?"

"Who should I tell her you are, since you don't look like you do in the photos?"

Johnny didn't have any other kids, not even with his current wife. Breeana was all he had.

"Tell her the truth and let me explain the rest."

She was hesitant, but she opened the door all

the way.

"You have one hour. It's almost her bedtime."

When he came in, Breeana somehow already knew who he was. In her mind, he still looked the same as the picture she kept by her nightstand.

"Daddy! Daddy!"

He lit up with a smile, followed by tears of happiness as he embraced her with a hug. He then felt regret for abandoning her.

"You were at work too long!" she said, since that is what she was told.

"I'm back now, and I hope to see more of you," he said. "Look what I got you."

He handed her the doll.

"Dora! Yeah! Mommy, look!"

Dawn came to tears, partially happy to see her daughter happy, but holding on to her anger against him for leaving her as well as her daughter.

"Daddy, you want to see my room? I have Dora everything."

"Let me ask Mommy if I can see your room." He turned to see Dawn crying. "You okay?"

"No and yeah. I don't know what to think or feel right now."

"Feel like me, Mommy," Breeana said, happy to see her father.

Dawn broke a smile through the emotional confusion.

Breeana took him by the hand and led him into the room.

"Come on, Daddy," she said innocently and full of life.

Dawn could not move. She was stuck in her position with her mind racing. This was the life she always wanted. She never wanted to raise Bree as a single mother. She always wanted him to be there making her happy like he was then.

No one cared about her or Bree until Juan came into her life. She could not abandon Juan. It would not be right, especially because it was what Johnny had done to her.

She could hear Bree talking away about showing him everything from her toys to her school work. This brought on even more pain. She wanted to know where he had been and why he had returned now.

Thirty minutes had gone by before Johnny came back out holding Bree. She was resting her head on his shoulder. She was Daddy's princess.

"I guess I'm about out of time?" he said.

"No, I want you to stay!" Bree said.

"Stay until she falls asleep," Dawn said, wanting to please her baby girl.

Bree was already tired, so it was just a matter of minutes before she fell asleep.

"Bree, I'm going to take you in the room while Mommy and I talk, okay?"

"Okay, make sure you come in and tuck me in."

"I will, princess."

After Breeana went into her room, Dawn was able to have a mature conversation. She discovered why he left and why he came back. He was in the process of getting a divorce from the same female with whom he cheated on her.

"So, you're going through this divorce, so you run back to me?"

"I'm running back to the one female that means the world to me and needs me in her life—and that's Breeana. It would be a plus if you took me back as well," he said with a smile.

She wasn't having him back only to allow him to hurt her again when the next female came along.

"I can't! I can't let you come back into my life and walk away when you feel like it. But you can see Bree. We can arrange something."

Johnny knew he had messed up, not just with his wife, but also with Dawn. He would do anything to come back into her life.

"You're right. Besides, I need to get my divorce final. By that time, I'll be able to prove to you I can be all you ever wanted."

She closed her eyes, and Juan's face flashed into her vision. With him there were good times and the promising future she envisioned, and a future in which Johnny was not a part.

"Just be here for your daughter. That's all that matters right now."

He stood up from the couch, leaving the subject alone and giving it the time, he thought he needed.

"Well, let me tuck her in."

He headed into Bree's room. She was asleep on top of the covers, and he picked her up and pulled the blanket and sheets back. Before laying her in the bed, he tucked her in, kissed her on the cheek, and then bowed his head in prayer.

Dawn was in the doorway viewing his fatherly ways, appreciating what he was doing for their daughter. He did not know she was behind him, until she spoke.

"Let yourself out. The bottom lock automatically locks."

He did not turn around since he was still in prayer. She headed to her bedroom to lie back down. She closed her eyes and thought about Juan. It was her way of combating the presence of Johnny and the old emotions.

Almost an hour passed by before Dawn got out of her bed to see if Johnny had left, because she did not hear the door open or shut. Or maybe she was just too far into her thoughts of Juan.

When she walked into Breeana's bedroom, Johnny was asleep on the side of her bed, resting his head on one of her stuffed animals. He did not have anywhere to go. His wife took over everything, which is why he flew to Pennsylvania, something he failed to share with Dawn. He had money, but he did not want to waste it on hotels.

A part of what she was watching was cute; however, at the same time, she knew he was far away from home. She turned back to her bedroom to lie back down, where she cuddled her pillow until she fell asleep.

Johnny woke up a half hour later and realized he had dozed off. He checked his watch, and it read 7:37 p.m. He made his way into the bathroom, and then came out with his clothes folded to perfection, ready for inspection as if he was still at the barracks.

He slipped into Dawn's room and saw that she was under the covers, so he pulled the blanket back a little and climbed into her bed, wearing only his boxer shorts and tank top.

He moved closer to her. Her back was turned, so he pressed his body up against hers, wrapping his arms around her. She did not resist. She was in dream mode. It was her fantasy world with Juan. Johnny placed a kiss on the back of her neck, and she moaned lightly. He was thinking that it was the kiss, but it was her thinking he was Juan.

She felt the firmness of Juan's body, which was really Johnny's body. His hands roamed her body and then tweaked her nipples before sliding down below and slipping his fingers into her panties to feel the silky hairs. He could not get in, so he turned her body to the side. He began kissing her cheek and then her lips. She still did not resist since she was so far in a dream state believing she was feeling Juan's lips.

She was now on her back with her pajama top raised up with his lips on her breast. His fingers now made their way into her panties, where he slid over her silky red hairs and then glided over the clitoris.

She loved this and did not want to wake up. This dream was more real than the fantasy in the shower. He rubbed her clitoris, which created a throbbing sensation that made her pant in her sleep.

"Mmmmh, mmmmh!"

He decided to part with his fingers one at a time into her tightness. He could not believe how tight it was, yet wet and warm. She squirmed and moaned as his finger moved in and out. Then he went for two fingers. But as he placed them inside, she moaned loudly and then her eyes came open. Seconds passed as she tried to zoom in on the face hoping it was Juan, not knowing that it was Johnny until she came to.

"Get off of me! What are you doing in my bed?"

He was shocked, thinking she liked it. He did not realize she did not know he was doing what he was doing to her.

She felt violated, even raped. She covered up her breasts. They were no longer for him, only Juan. She was not a whore or some baby momma where he could show up any time. She was a faithful woman to whatever man was lucky enough to have her, and this was Juan.

She jumped out of the bed.

"I said get out right now! You come in here with your slick shit! I don't want you!"

He got out of the bed and quickly put on his clothes.

"I'm sorry, but what the hell are you snapping for? I thought you liked that?"

"I was asleep, dumb ass! Now get out!"

He walked out of the room, and she followed behind him. This time she would make sure he left.

She opened the front door and waved him out.

"You're no longer welcome here, unless it's daytime hours. If you don't like that, get a lawyer and we can schedule your visits!"

She slammed the door, locked it, and then headed to the shower. But she first stopped off at Bree's room, where she found her daughter was still sound asleep. Thank God, Dawn thought.

Dawn made her way into the shower after feeling violated.

As the water beat down on her body, she cried and wished Juan was there to comfort her. She also wished that what she was feeling was his touch instead of her creepy ex-fiancé's.

Chapter 14

*D*eja pulled up to the five-star Warren Charles restaurant at 8:15 p.m. in her lipstick-red Audi S5 sports coupe with the Puerto Rican flag on the front plate.

Dinner was scheduled at 7:30 p.m., and she was there at 7:45; however, she did manage to call Tom to make him aware of her being a little late to get her hair together. She also made sure she looked good, which was something that she did with ease. Even the valet attendant took notice as she stepped out of her car wearing tan Vera Wang stilettos, that gave her short frame a little height while pushing her curvy bum up, that fit perfectly into her thigh-high white D & G dress, the same dress she saw Kim Kardashian wear on the red carpet. Deja's wrist also sparkled with the diamond bracelet that Tom had purchased, along with the earrings she had treated herself with. Her hair was pulled back to display all of her natural beauty and exotic features. She also carried a small Gucci clutch that complemented her head-to-toe look.

When she entered the restaurant, she stopped to speak to the maitre d'.

"Excuse me, but I'm here for a 7:30 with Tom Jones."

The maitre d' already knew that Mr. Jones was expecting her. In fact, he directed Deja to the table.

"Yes, ma'am, come with me."

Tom had secured a private table set in a secluded partition to give them their much-needed privacy while still highlighting the view of illuminated downtown Harrisburg and the Susquehanna River.

Deja had never been to a five-star restaurant, so when Tom told her he was treating her to this place, she went online to do a little research, which made her want to come looking sexy and dinner formal. She was definitely doing both, looking as if she was Hollywood elite.

She was scanned as she walked through the restaurant. Even the men on dates with their wives and girlfriends checked her out.

A lot of important people were there, she thought. Everyone looked like they had money or was someone with status. The cars in front also provided proof that this was not like the places Juan had taken her to.

"Mr. Jones, your guest has arrived," the maitre d' announced.

"Thank you, Alfred," Tom said as he stood up wowed by Deja's appearance. She was ten times sexier than she was at the mall. "You look exotic in a good way; in fact, stunning, to be exact. Now I know what took so long. It was worth the wait."

"Gracias, papi. You look handsome, like a

model in *GQ* magazine."

Tom was wearing a tailored grey suit made by Sean Jean with initialed platinum cufflinks that matched the limited-edition platinum Rolex Presidential with a pearl face and black Gucci soft leather shoes. He looked the part of a young self-made millionaire who was finally treating himself to the good life.

"Let me get your seat, beautiful," he said as he came around to her side of the table to seat her.

"Thank you. I never had someone pull out my chair or take me to a nice place like this."

"This is life for me, and for the one who comes into my life who's willing to share all of this with me." He pointed around when speaking.

She lit up with a smile before asking, "What do you mean 'all of this,' the restaurant?"

He was preparing to speak, when the servers

came; one took orders for the bar, while the other took the meal order.

"Mr. Jones, here's the wine and beverage menu," the server said before he stepped back to allow the other server to present the other menu.

"Mr. Jones, the dinner menu. Would you care to hear the chef's special this evening?" the server asked, first looking at Tom and then Deja.

"Please, my guest may be willing to try something new," Tom said, using his words as a pun, hoping she knew what he was saying.

"Freshly imported soft-shell crabs seasoned with a creamy garlic Mornay sauce and garnished with imported truffles."

"Thank you, Simone. Please give us a minute or so and come back," he said as the beverage server still stood waiting.

"Could I get you anything to drink while you think about your dinner order?"

Deja did not know what she should order. Normally she would get something like a Corona, but this was not the place for that.

"Apple martini, please," she said softly, displaying a shy side.

"The usual for you, Mr. Jones?"

"Yes, Demitri."

Deja took in everything, including the three forks, two spoons, and three knives. The only time she had seen this much silverware was in a kitchen drawer. Soft white cotton cloths were elegant, and the lighting was even perfect—not too bright or too dim, but low, just as the music playing in the background.

As she looked at the menu, she noticed there were no prices, which was another first for her.

"I take it you come here a lot since you have a regular drink, and everyone knows you by name?"

"Actually, beautiful, I own this place."

"Since you own this place, tell me why there aren't prices on the menu."

He laughed loving her innocence and demeanor. She was real. Most women that were not used to this lifestyle would have at least faked it, which was something he did not want any woman to do around him. Because to him, faking it was just like being deceptive.

"The people that come here can afford to eat here, so putting a price on something they want to eat is not necessary."

"I would get a steak, but that would be the norm for me."

"The steaks here are also imported. They're Kobe beef, so it may not be your normal cut of steak."

Demitri returned with the drinks.

"Apple martini for the lady."

"Thank you. This looks good," Deja said while looking at the fancy glass trimming and cherry.

"Double Cîroc with a twist of lemon, no ice."

Demitri also set down two glasses of spring water with lemon slices.

"Will that be all for now, Mr. Jones?"

"Yes, that will be all for now."

Simone appeared after Demitri left.

"Are we ready to place orders? Any appetizers?"

"I know what I want now," Deja said. "I would like to try something new," she emphasized with a smile. "The chef's special."

She made eye contact with Tom, who appeared a bit surprised by her choice.

"Great choice! We also have a fresh spinach leaf salad with the chef's signature dressing to complement the meal, or you could choose another salad?"

"I'll take what the chef recommends."

"What will you be having tonight, sir?"

"The Kobe porterhouse, Caesar salad, and baked potato with melted garlic butter."

"The steak medium as usual, sir?"

"Yes! Also, when the meals come, have Demitri bring another round of drinks."

"I sure will, sir."

"You trying to get me drunk or something? I do have to drive."

"You're a big girl. Besides, if you don't wish to drive, I'll get you home."

She smiled, thinking to herself what his intent was.

"Remember, this is only a date to show you my appreciation for buying this nice bracelet."

"Speaking of bracelet, you make it look good the way you're wearing it. You know how to dress."

She was almost done with her drink and ready to have another. At the same time, she was ready to eat. The aroma of fine cuisine was in the air.

"Since this is an appreciation date as you said, allow me to get to know more about you—who Deja really is. Therefore, I cannot only say I've seen the most beautiful woman, but I also got a chance to know who she is."

Tom was smooth the way he formed his words, and his delivery and timing were even better. He placed a smile not just on her face, but also in her eyes. They sparkled, and the way she was feeling in the moment was different than the way she was with Juan. Also, a part of her questioned why she should have to rebuild when she could start fresh with someone new, something meant to be, or something special and unique.

"I'm partially obligated, as I told you earlier."

Tom knew that was not a sign of promise, so he kept that in his thoughts.

"However, when I am with someone who is

100 percent into me, I give them the same in return. I like the institution of being in a relationship, and knowing you have someone who's going to have your back and be your comfort when you need them. I guess you can say I'm a sucker for love, a true romantic?"

She paused to finish off her drink, and then took the cherry and pressed it against her soft lips before briefly sticking out her tongue, playing with it, and finally eating it.

"Mmm, good. I'm a Scorpio born on November 18th. I'm the only child and spoiled a little."

"A little?" Tom said with a smirk. "From the way you look, you like to have it your way."

"I did this for you," she quickly responded, not wanting him to know she really did go all out for him, but it slipped.

"I cherish your presence as well as what you did to make this night special thus far for me."

Dinner arrived and smelled good.

"Soft-shell crabs for the lady with a fresh spinach salad."

"Wow, papi! This looks too good to eat, but I'm going to eat, trust me. I'm hungry. I didn't eat all day, so I could look good in this dress."

Tom started laughing because she was uncensored and real.

"That's what I like about you, you speak the truth."

"Your steak, sir."

The food was placed on the table, and then Demitri removed the empty glasses with their fresh drinks.

Deja started on her food and loved the Mornay sauce and the freshly imported crabs.

"Ah, Dios mio! I love this! This is going to be my new favorite thing," she said while chewing what she had in her mouth before taking her fork and pressing into the soft-shell crab to serve a piece for Tom. "Taste it, papi."

Tom leaned in close with his mouth open to take in the flavorful crab.

"Mmmmmh, this is good! I may have to give the chef a raise for making me look good," Tom joked.

He cut into his steak and placed a piece on the fork for her.

"Now it's time you tried something new. This beef is the best in the world."

She laughed at how he said it and what he was saying. Then it came to him what he just had said about the beef.

"Thoughtful, but I wasn't meaning it like that," he said, reaching for his fork with the medium Kobe steak.

Her mouth opened as she wrapped her lips around the cut of steak. She closed her eyes and savored the moment while making it look good.

"Mmm hmmmmh! This melts in your

mouth."

"Like chocolate M & M's melt in your mouth?" he said with pun intended, making her laugh once more.

The night was going very well. The two conversed, ate, and drank as the time passed them by. They were both caught up in the moment of goodness, and she even managed to consume a few more apple martinis.

Being the gentleman that Tom was, he decided to call it a night and bring the dinner date to an end.

"Demitri! Simone! Your service tonight was on point," Tom said, leaving each of the servers a $100 bill. "View it as a bonus for your services."

"Thank you, Mr. Jones."

Tom reached out for Deja's hand. She stood from her seat feeling the martinis, but she remained a lady aware of her surroundings.

"You know I can't drive right now!" Deja said.

"You don't have to," he said, leading the way out of the front.

His car and chauffeur awaited them. He owned an all-black pearl Rolls Royce Phantom, with hand-crafted black leather seats and 9-inch screens in the headrest for his viewing pleasure.

"You want my driver to take you to your place?" Tom asked, still being a gentleman.

Deja did not want to go home. She wanted to see more of this affluent lifestyle. She was intrigued by Tom. There was more to him than the money; besides, she did not want to roll up to her apartment building in this $500,000 car.

"I want to come with you, unless you're trying to get rid of me?" she said sarcastically.

"Now why would I want to do a thing like that?" he answered, allowing her to get in the Phantom first.

He slid into the luxury vehicle and wrapped his arm around Deja while waiting on the driver to get in.

"To my place, Wilson."

Tom resided in Pinehurst, a multi-million-dollar sumptuous estate, with mansions boasting four- and five-car garages, pools, privacy, home theaters, gyms, and spas, along with all the other customized amenities of a millionaire.

She felt like she was in a fairy tale or a movie star being whisked away in the luxury vehicle.

The cabin was quiet as the Phantom drove. Deja snuggled up against Tom and took it all in while looking through the dark tint at the stars in the sky pass by. Within minutes, they arrived at the gated community.

Deja sat up and looked at the mansions, the landscape, the lighting, the flawless brickwork on some of the mansions, and the multiple garages that each estate boasted.

She had never seen anything like this other than watching *MTV Cribs* or in the movies.

The chauffeur pulled up the long driveway to the front of the 8,000-square-foot estate that housed five garages.

"We're here, Mr. Jones," Wilson said, just in case Tom was sleeping.

Wilson came around to open the door.

"Will you be needing my services anymore tonight, sir?"

"No, I'm in for the night."

Tom led Deja by the hand into his open foyer with the crystal chandelier hanging twenty feet above and reflecting on the marble floor.

"Can I get the MTV Crib tour?" Deja asked, being funny and real.

"The pleasure will be all mine, beautiful."

He took her through the first floor, wowing her in every room. She came into the living room with the chinchilla rug as a centerpiece. Most chinchilla coats cost upward of $50,000, so she knew the carpet was expensive. She took off her shoes and stepped on the soft centerpiece.

"This feels good. It's like a massage on my feet!"

Tom laughed at how innocently she reacted.

She got down on the floor to feel the softness with her hands. It was almost stimulating.

"Let's go see the rest of the place. We can always come back to this room whenever you like."

She loved the sound of the invitation to return.

He took her to the lower level, where the estate flaunted a home theater, game room, gym, and spa.

They ended up at the spa last, which really wowed her.

"So you be up in here giving people massages?"

"Not that I don't know how to, but I have people that come in for that."

She hopped up on the massage table with her bare feet dangling as she swayed them back and forth, all the while eyeing him down with a salacious look in her eyes.

"Practice makes perfect!" she said while extending her foot for a massage.

He smiled as he reached for her foot.

"So, you do like to be spoiled and have it your way?"

She responded with her eyes sparkling, which told a story in itself.

"That feels good too. Don't forget the other foot," she said, raising it up and rubbing against him.

"For you showing up looking as good as you did tonight, I'll be your servant. Your wish is my command. Hold on a sec. I have something special for this massage."

He made his way over to the cabinet and took out the lavender scented oil. He heated it up to the perfect temperature and then lit a few candles around the spa to set the mood.

"Now if you like, I would love to give you a full-body hot-oil massage. No sex, just a friendly passionate massage?"

"What woman would resist such an offer, and sex-free?"

"No sex, just a massage."

She hopped back off the table. She then slid out of her dress and exposed her smooth Puerto Rican skin, flat stomach, curves in all the right places, and white lace bra-and-panty set from Victoria's Secret. She removed the bra and panty and showed her landing strip, before turning around and hopping back up on the table.

"You want to hear some music?" he asked.

"Tre Songz? Ne-Yo? Day 26? Any of them. You know, something slow?"

Tom stepped over to the digital stereo system and punched in the names of the artists she requested. He then pushed Play All.

The first CD was Tre Songz's "Making Love Faces."

She was lying face down on her stomach on the massage table.

Tom took off his clothing down to his boxers and tank top since he did not want to ruin his expensive attire.

He started on her calves with the hot oil, pouring a little at a time and making her feel good. His masculine hands and fingers pressed deep into her flesh to relax her muscles. Her eyes were closed as she embraced what was happening to her and loving every minute of it.

Tom moved up to her thighs, deep tissue massaging them. His fingers moved close to her landing strip, but he did not touch it. He then moved to her butt, pressing deep with his thumbs as she moaned in pleasure. She had never had this done before. Tom climbed onto the table to have a better position as he pressed his thumbs into the small of her back, up her spine, back down her sides, then back up to the shoulders and to her neck. He applied more hot oil, which assisted the passionate massage.

Next, his fingers and hands worked down her back. This time his lips made their way kissing down her spine and sending a sensual chill down her back. She loved it and did not complain at all. The kisses continued down to the small of her back and over her butt, where he kissed each cheek as his fingers massaged deeply. He then parted her legs while still massaging and kissing her. He placed a kiss to her love spot as she moaned. She wanted more. He continued kissing down her thighs while still pressing into her flesh with his fingers massaging her body. He returned to her cheeks and massaged them as he went back in to kiss her love spot again.

His lips pressed against her love spot passionately. She moaned again as her fluids flowed. She wanted him to continue. She was hot and heating up by the second, the more he touched her. His hands continued to massage as he went in for another kiss to the kitty.

"Ahi, papi, stop teasing me!" she pleaded, wanting his lips on her kitty.

He halted the massage since he needed his fingers to assist the magic. He then parted her love spot while thrusting his tongue in and out while she squirmed. She loved it as she tried to contain her sexual excitement. This was the real thing, and something she had not had in over seven months.

His tongue found her clitoris, which set her off moaning wildly.

"Ahi, ahi! Mmmmh, mmmmmh! Ahi, papi,

ahi, papi."

His fingers assisted thrusting in and out while his tongue pinned down the clitoris. Her body was overwhelmed with sensation. Something was happening to her that she never had experienced with Juan: Tom was older, and he knew the woman's body. He was good. Her legs started trembling as her moans became louder.

"I'm cumming! Mmmmmh! Aaaaaaah!"

His tongue went faster, just as his fingers did. Her legs clenched, and her moans became steady. She then sighed as she released from multiple orgasms. She could no longer move! Tom's tongue was still going, and her body was exploding with pleasure. He was giving her the best oral experience she ever had. He stopped and then started back up with the massage, kissing her back until he made his way up to her neck.

"You like this massage, beautiful?" he asked in a low whisper while still kissing her body.

"I think this was more than a massage, but I love it, papi!"

Tom was not pressed to have intercourse with her, because he was looking into the future. There would be another time. In this case, he planned to make her his woman.

Sexually, Deja was more than satisfied, and she looked forward to this type of treatment more often.

Tom was kissing her shoulders and loving every part of her, when she added, "Would you always be good to me?"

The multiple orgasms had her open emotionally, and she allowed him to have a part of her. She deserved an answer.

Tom was taken aback that she initiated such a question, and this in itself made him place her on a pedestal.

"You like to be spoiled, and you like to have it your way, so I don't think I have a choice other than to be good to you," he said with a big grin.

"If it makes you feel better, I can let you have it your way and spoil you too."

"I could get used to being your love slave, and, in return, you can cater to me the same."

She turned over and looked up into his eyes. She wanted to see the man she was falling for—the man that made her feel and experience the multiples and open her up to such emotion.

"You want me?" she questioned sounding heartfelt.

At first he was thinking she meant sexually.

"No sex, remember?"

"Not like that. Do you want me in your life? Or is this just something you do because you can afford to do it?"

Tom not only appreciated her the more she spoke, but he was also falling for her personality, because she spoke what she thought and felt.

"I want you! I want to be able to wake up to you every day if possible. It gets lonely in here knowing I finally have the wealth but no love. So if you would do me the honor of being the one I share my life with, then I am more than thankful for you coming into my life."

"No, you came into my life at the jewelry store!" she reminded him.

"Let's say fate brought us together."

"And falling in love with you will keep us together," she responded with her eyes full of passion.

He leaned in to kiss her soft lips while their warm bodies embraced. It was fate being in the right place at the right time.

"Let's head upstairs, get showered up, and get some rest. I have a flight to Miami to catch in the morning."

He gathered their things and then helped her off the massage table.

They made their way into the hallway to the elevator that led up to the second floor, where the master bedroom was located. The suite also housed the large his-and-her bathrooms with attached walk-in closets.

"This is your shower, and my shower is over there. On the days you want to join me, feel free."

She laughed at him and felt so good inside. She felt like a princess.

After the shower, they made their way into the large suite under the navy-blue satin sheets.

"Good night, papi," she said in a sexy, loving voice.

"Good night, beautiful," he responded, kissing her forehead and then her lips before lying back, closing his eyes, and appreciating her being the one.

She snuggled up next to him, feeling her heart opening up and falling for him. It was a new start and a new beginning to a new love. She was not about to let him get away or ruin a good thing.

All she had to worry about now was how to let Juan down . . . again.

Part 2 Now Available

Text Good2Go at 31996 to receive new release updates via text message.

PMC © 12172001-2-7-2011
A W.C. Holloway Story

To order books, please fill out the order form below:
To order films please go to www.good2gofilms.com

Name: __ _____

Address:_____

City: _____ State: _____ Zip Code: _____

Phone:_____

Email:_____

Method of Payment: Check   VISA   MASTERCARD

Credit Card#:_ _____

Name as it appears on card: _____

Signature: _____

Item Name	Price	Qty	Amount
48 Hours to Die – Silk White	$14.99		
A Hustler's Dream - Ernest Morris	$14.99		
A Hustler's Dream 2 - Ernest Morris	$14.99		
A Thug's Devotion – J. L. Rose and J. M. McMillon	$14.99		
All Eyes on Tommy Gunz – Warren Holloway	$14.99		
Black Reign – Ernest Morris	$14.99		
Bloody Mayhem Down South – Trayvon Jackson	$14.99		
Bloody Mayhem Down South 2 – Trayvon Jackson	$14.99		
Business Is Business – Silk White	$14.99		
Business Is Business 2 – Silk White	$14.99		
Business Is Business 3 – Silk White	$14.99		
Childhood Sweethearts – Jacob Spears	$14.99		
Childhood Sweethearts 2 – Jacob Spears	$14.99		
Childhood Sweethearts 3 - Jacob Spears	$14.99		
Childhood Sweethearts 4 - Jacob Spears	$14.99		
Connected To The Plug – Dwan Marquis Williams	$14.99		
Connected To The Plug 2 – Dwan Marquis Williams	$14.99		
Connected To The Plug 3 – Dwan Williams	$14.99		
Deadly Reunion – Ernest Morris	$14.99		
Dream's Life – Assa Raymond Baker	$14.99		
Flipping Numbers – Ernest Morris	$14.99		
Flipping Numbers 2 – Ernest Morris	$14.99		
He Loves Me, He Loves You Not - Mychea	$14.99		
He Loves Me, He Loves You Not 2 - Mychea	$14.99		
He Loves Me, He Loves You Not 3 - Mychea	$14.99		
He Loves Me, He Loves You Not 4 – Mychea	$14.99		
He Loves Me, He Loves You Not 5 – Mychea	$14.99		

Lord of My Land – Jay Morrison	$14.99		
Lost and Turned Out – Ernest Morris	$14.99		
Love Hates Violence – De'Wayne Maris	$14.99		
Married To Da Streets – Silk White	$14.99		
M.E.R.C. - Make Every Rep Count Health and Fitness	$14.99		
Money Make Me Cum – Ernest Morris	$14.99		
My Besties – Asia Hill	$14.99		
My Besties 2 – Asia Hill	$14.99		
My Besties 3 – Asia Hill	$14.99		
My Besties 4 – Asia Hill	$14.99		
My Boyfriend's Wife - Mychea	$14.99		
My Boyfriend's Wife 2 – Mychea	$14.99		
My Brothers Envy – J. L. Rose	$14.99		
My Brothers Envy 2 – J. L. Rose	$14.99		
Naughty Housewives – Ernest Morris	$14.99		
Naughty Housewives 2 – Ernest Morris	$14.99		
Naughty Housewives 3 – Ernest Morris	$14.99		
Naughty Housewives 4 – Ernest Morris	$14.99		
Never Be The Same – Silk White	$14.99		
Shades of Revenge – Assa Raymond Baker	$14.99		
Slumped – Jason Brent	$14.99		
Someone's Gonna Get It – Mychea	$14.99		
Stranded – Silk White	$14.99		
Supreme & Justice – Ernest Morris	$14.99		
Supreme & Justice 2 – Ernest Morris	$14.99		
Supreme & Justice 3 – Ernest Morris	$14.99		
Tears of a Hustler - Silk White	$14.99		
Tears of a Hustler 2 - Silk White	$14.99		
Tears of a Hustler 3 - Silk White	$14.99		
Tears of a Hustler 4- Silk White	$14.99		
Tears of a Hustler 5 – Silk White	$14.99		
Tears of a Hustler 6 – Silk White	$14.99		
The Last Love Letter – Warren Holloway	$14.99		
The Last Love Letter 2 – Warren Holloway	$14.99		

THE LAST LOVE LETTER

The Panty Ripper - Reality Way	$14.99		
The Panty Ripper 3 – Reality Way	$14.99		
The Solution – Jay Morrison	$14.99		
The Teflon Queen – Silk White	$14.99		
The Teflon Queen 2 – Silk White	$14.99		
The Teflon Queen 3 – Silk White	$14.99		
The Teflon Queen 4 – Silk White	$14.99		
The Teflon Queen 5 – Silk White	$14.99		
The Teflon Queen 6 - Silk White	$14.99		
The Vacation – Silk White	$14.99		
Tied To A Boss - J.L. Rose	$14.99		
Tied To A Boss 2 - J.L. Rose	$14.99		
Tied To A Boss 3 - J.L. Rose	$14.99		
Tied To A Boss 4 - J.L. Rose	$14.99		
Tied To A Boss 5 - J.L. Rose	$14.99		
Time Is Money - Silk White	$14.99		
Tomorrow's Not Promised – Robert Torres	$14.99		
Tomorrow's Not Promised 2 – Robert Torres	$14.99		
Two Mask One Heart – Jacob Spears and Trayvon Jackson	$14.99		
Two Mask One Heart 2 – Jacob Spears and Trayvon Jackson	$14.99		
Two Mask One Heart 3 – Jacob Spears and Trayvon Jackson	$14.99		
Wrong Place Wrong Time – Silk White	$14.99		
Young Goonz – Reality Way	$14.99		
Subtotal:			
Tax:			
Shipping (Free) U.S. Media Mail:			
Total:			

Make Checks Payable To:
Good2Go Publishing
7311 W Glass Lane,
Laveen, AZ 85339